A.K.A. Suzette

Lois Jean Thomas

This book is a work of fiction. Names, characters, places, and incidents are the product of the author's imagination or are used fictitiously. Any resemblance between events, locales, or persons, living or dead, is coincidental.

ISBN-13: 978-0-9910749-6-9

Library of Congress Control Number: 2014922129
Lois Jean Thomas, Saint Joseph, Michigan

This book is fondly dedicated to my home community of Brown County, Indiana. No matter where I've traveled in life, my roots are still here.

While all the events, the characters and their residences, and some of the businesses are entirely figments of my imagination, this story is physically grounded in Nashville, Indiana, and the surrounding communities.

CONTENTS

ACKNOWLEDGMENTS

As always, I'd like to express my deepest gratitude to my husband Allen for his endless patience and kind support in helping me format this book.

A special thanks to my sister Rachel Roberts and my friend Mary Ruth Fox, who provided some of the details used in creating the setting for this story.

And a big thank you to the members of Writers' Bloc: Marnie, Judy, Sue, Anne, Richard, Elaine, Ron, and Isabel. Your feedback helped make this a better story.

A.K.A. Suzette

CHAPTER 1

Not many people would think Suzette deserves to have her story told. Some people I know would turn up their snooty noses and say she isn't worth the paper and ink it takes to make a book. Well, to heck with them. I'm going to tell it anyway. I need to.

I can't explain how my friendship with Suzette was forged, except to say that she took me captive. At first, she made me nervous, and I tried to steer clear of her. But over time, I learned to enjoy her company, and later, I became jealous when others stole her attention away from me.

Normally, you never would have found me at Buck's Dance Hall, where I first met Suzette. I was too shy for places like that, especially going on my own. But that day, I was forcing myself to branch out.

I'd never done much branching out, having lived my entire life under the thumb of my illustrious grandmother, Arlene Greene, president of the Brown County Historical Society, member of Nashville's town council, patron of the Brown County Art Guild.

And I shared that tiny under-the-thumb space with my mild-mannered mother, who was only eighteen years my senior. Once when I was a child, I overheard my mom's friend say, "Vivien, your mother keeps you in a feather prison."

"I don't think that's the case," came back my mother's weak retort.

But her friend's strange words had a ring of truth to them. They stuck in my mind, and the older I grew, the more I understood the meaning of that type of confinement.

Like when Nana threw lavish birthday parties for me, ordering beautifully decorated chocolate cakes from the IGA bakery, even thought I hated chocolate and always asked for white. She'd invite her friends and their grandchildren, uppity children who snubbed me even at my own parties, rather than the ordinary kids I hung around with on the playground of Nashville Elementary School.

Nana didn't know how to live outside the spotlight, so the parties were ever and always about her. When I was seven, I sneaked out of the house and disappeared into our wooded backyard during my own birthday party, without her even noticing. Wearing only my pale pink party dress, I climbed a tulip poplar tree and huddled in the curve between two branches, shivering in the November chill, waiting for Nana's show to be over.

After a while, my mother came out. "Come back inside, Elaine," she said. "Nana's ready to serve the cake." I slipped while I was climbing down, and skinned my leg. My mother caught me, and held me like she understood while I allowed myself to cry a little bit. Then she set me down, took me by the hand, and dutifully led me back into the house.

And there were those times in my teenage years when Nana bought me pastel sweaters from the high-end stores in nearby Columbus, costly, well-made sweaters meant for classy women much older than me. Everything in my wardrobe ended up pale. I always gravitated toward vibrant colors, bright pinks and reds, but Nana said they overpowered my fair complexion. So what choice did I have but to wear her expensive pallid purchases, to stand out as a dork in the world of my trendy peers?

The year Nana bought my mother and me matching baby-blue cardigans, I was baffled and strangely hurt, for reasons I didn't understand. I pondered on my wounded feelings in the privacy of my bedroom, surrounded by floral-papered walls on which I couldn't possibly hang a poster of a screaming rock star. And it came to me that for Nana, my mother and I blended into one blob of a spineless personality, the personality it was her responsibility to protect, to provide for, and to control.

But pastel colors weren't meant for Arlene Greene. Her snazzy jewel-tone pantsuits somehow made her big-busted, big-bellied figure look regal. Her oversized rhinestone-studded red-framed eyeglasses would have looked garish on anyone else, but they suited her perfectly, nicely accenting her smooth golden-tan skin, her plump, pretty features, and her fluffy blonde hairdo.

No, there wasn't much room under Nana's thumb, and certainly no room for male influence. Up until the point of my marriage, I knew no other world than living with my mother and Nana in our well-kept, wood-sided ranch home on Artist Drive in the small town of Nashville, Indiana. Granted, my grandfather, a dentist, was there for awhile, but he died when I was five. He was colorless wisp of a man, a distant and shadowy figure who scarcely made an imprint on my memory. He didn't have a chance to impress me, because my robust grandmother outshone, outweighed, and overpowered him.

And of course, I never knew my father. When I was four, I asked my mother, "Do I have a daddy?"

She looked startled, and while she fumbled for words, Nana jumped in and said, "Of course you do, Elaine. All children have daddies. But yours is dead."

That news jolted me and kept me quiet for awhile, but some months later, I came to my mother with another question, this time when Nana was out of earshot. "Did my daddy love me?"

"He didn't have a chance to love you," my mother said nervously. "He never knew you. He died before you were born."

Over the years, I pieced together what scanty information I could glean about my father. When I was six, I learned that he'd been killed when he was struck by a pickup truck. When I was eight, I learned that this dreadful event happened when he was working on a road construction crew.

My heart longed to know more about my daddy, but my mind began to settle for the idea that having an absent, mystery-shrouded father was a normal part of childhood.

CHAPTER 2

On an April day when I was twelve, I finally stumbled upon the goldmine of information I'd been waiting for.

Every spring, Nana picked a Sunday afternoon to take my mother and me on a hike across the hilly, winding Freeman Ridge, so that we could enjoy the splendor of Brown County's dogwood and redbud trees in bloom. "Our little family tradition," she called it.

She'd drive us to the ridge the long way around, north on State Road 135 to Bean Blossom, then several miles east on Gatesville Road. Then she'd carefully ease her big car up the steep, narrow Bear Wallow Hill Road. Just over the top of the hill, the road connected with our destination, the east end of Freeman Ridge.

Jack and Opal Reinhardt lived in a tiny cottage near the top of Bear Wallow Hill. For years, Nana had a standing agreement with the Reinhardts that she could park her car in their driveway while we took our hike. As a gesture of appreciation for their kindness, she'd knock on their door and deliver a plate of cookies or cupcakes to the elderly couple. After Jack died, Nana continued to carry her annual offering of sweet treats to his frail octogenarian widow.

After we'd dutifully hike as far across the ridge as Nana thought we should, we'd turn back and retrieve our car from the Reinhardts' driveway. Then Nana would drive the short route home, down the full length of the ridge to where the west end converged with Greasy Creek Road just before it intersected with State Road 135.

But on the day designated for my twelfth annual ridge hike, Nana's back ached and the bunions caused by squeezing her fat feet into tight pumps were bothering her. Sinking into her leather Lazy-Boy recliner, she waved her hand and said, "You two go ahead." Then she pointed toward the kitchen. "Vivien, don't forget Opal's cheesecake. It's in the refrigerator. She's expecting you."

Feeling strangely free, my mother and I climbed into Nana's Buick and headed north toward Bean Blossom. It occurred to me that we could have ditched Nana's plans and done something of our own choosing. But neither of us was given to duplicity, and disposing of Opal's cheesecake and later telling Nana a boldfaced lie was beyond any form of rebellion we could conceive of.

However, instead of passing by the west ends of Freeman Ridge and Greasy Creek Road on our way to Gatesville Road, my mother slowed the car and said, "I think I'll drive up this way." I turned my head to look out the window, hiding my smile.

After delivering the cheesecake, we strolled the short distance down Bear Wallow Hill before turning onto the narrow, unpaved wooded ridge. In the past, Nana had been the self-designated party to point out the dogwood and redbud trees to her clueless companions. "Look over there," she'd say to my mother and me, as if we weren't capable of noticing anything on our own.

But that Sunday afternoon, unencumbered by Nana's overbearing presence, my mother and I spontaneously moved into a lighthearted game of seeing who could first spot the exotic trees that were playing hide-and-seek with us. We giggled when we called out in unison, "There's a dogwood tree!" Occasionally, my mother commented on the loveliness of the rustic dwellings nestled in the hills, the country escapes of the city-weary wealthy.

Suddenly, she pointed to a cabin set back off the road, a

shabby little place that appeared to be vacant. "Your father and I checked out that cabin when we were trying to find a place to rent," she said, a wistful look in her eyes.

My mother's unexpected revelation startled me. We'd walked that trail with Nana a dozen times, and she'd never pointed out that cabin before. But I knew why. For years, I'd sensed that Nana made every effort to erase from our family history the account of my mother's involvement with my father.

"Did you live there?" I asked.

"No," she said. "We couldn't afford it. It looks trashy now, but back then, it was really cute. The landlord was asking too much money, and we couldn't make it on my income alone."

For as long as I could remember, my mother had worked as a teller at the National City Bank in Nashville. I didn't figure she earned much money, but she didn't need to, as Nana took care of everything. I'd never faced the issue of money shortage. After my grandfather died, Nana had sold his dental practice, and that, combined with Grandpa's shrewd investments and a sizable life-insurance policy, kept Nana, my mother, and me living in modest comfort.

"Didn't my dad make money?" I asked.

My mother furrowed her brow and bit her lip, as if trying to decide how to phrase her response. "Well," she finally said, "for a few weeks, he had a job at Cummins in Columbus. He was making pretty good money, but then he got fired. Nana got mad and said she wasn't going to help us. She said that if we wanted to be married, we had to make it on our own." Her voice trailed off, and the sorrow weighing down her delicate features made her look haggard.

"Why did he get fired?" I asked.

My mother began to speak with an unusual urgency, her words pouring out from some deep source she couldn't dam up. "Because he was an independent kind of guy. He didn't like taking orders from anyone. That just wasn't his nature. Nana didn't understand that. When he lost his job at Cummins, she gave him all kinds of hell."

My soft-spoken mother's use of crude language shocked me, but I said nothing, letting her plunge ahead. "So he signed up to work on a road crew, just to get her off his back, and three days into the job, he got hit by a truck and was killed."

Suddenly, she seemed exhausted, on the verge of collapse, and she leaned her back against the massive trunk of a hickory tree for support. I stood transfixed, staring into her tortured face. The bitterness in her voice and the way she'd phrased what she'd just told me sounded like she thought Nana had set my father up to get killed. But I knew she'd never say such a thing outright, not in a million years.

"Where did it happen?" I asked.

"On State Road 46, between Nashville and Bloomington. I never like taking that route to Bloomington. I hate passing that spot. You know those signs that say anyone who kills a worker will get fined? Well, the driver of that pickup truck had to pay a big fat fine. I'm glad, because he killed my husband. He shouldn't have gotten away with that."

She'd begun to choke on her words, and I knew she was too distraught to talk any longer. Taking her hand, I said, "Let's go back."

In the silent cocoon of our shared grief, my mother and I walked the half-mile back to Opal's driveway. But as we approached our car, I had to ask one more question. "Do I look like my father?"

She glanced sideways at me. "Not much."

I knew she was telling me the truth, because I was very nearly a carbon-copy of her: slight build, thin face, a short, straight nose, deep-set blue eyes, full lips, and light brown hair that went limp in the southern Indiana humidity.

Then she smiled and caressed the back of my hand with her thumb. "You have his hands."

I extricated my hand from hers and stared at it, the strong, square hand that seemed a bit out of sync with the rest of my skinny frame.

"Do you have any pictures of him?" I asked.

"I think so," she said, her voice unusually tender.

When we got home, my mother went straight to her bedroom and closed the door. Later in the day, she caught me when Nana wasn't around and pressed an old, creased photograph into my hand. "This was taken on our wedding day," she said. "We got married in a pavilion in Brown County State Park."

I slipped into my own room to study the first photo I'd ever seen of my father. The tall, sturdily built young man wearing jeans and a short-sleeved shirt couldn't have been more than eighteen or nineteen.

I was momentarily puzzled, unable to connect his casual attire with the occasion of a wedding. Then my reasoning told me that Nana had refused to have anything to do with that distasteful event, and that the affair has been planned by teenagers who had no money and who hardly knew what they were doing.

I searched my father's face for features that resembled mine, but found none, and the hands that supposedly looked like mine were shoved into his pockets. His thick, brown, unkempt hair hung to his shoulders, and his dark, unsmiling eyes stared intently at the camera. It was hard to tell whether those penetrating eyes signified keen intelligence or an indomitable spirit, but I was pretty sure that my mother's involvement with my father was her one and only walk on the wild side.

I turned the photo over and saw the name *Travis McCoy* written on the back. It occurred to me that I hadn't even been allowed to keep his last name, and a wave of sadness washed over me. Somehow, my mother and I had reverted to using her maiden name of Greene. Nana's doings, no doubt.

Under my father's name was written, *May 13, 1978*, a date exactly six months prior to the day of my birth. I felt my body sag as another huge piece of the puzzle fell into place.

Over the next few years, I asked other questions about my father. My mother repeatedly said, "I can't tell you everything you want to know, Elaine. We were together for only a few months."

Once, I asked about grandparents on my father's side. "I don't know anything about them," my mother said. "I never met anyone in his family, except for his brother."

"Where's his brother now?" I asked, visions of meeting a long-lost uncle flashing through my mind.

"I don't know," she said. "After your father died, his brother arranged to have his body taken back to Kentucky, where they came from. I haven't heard anything from him since then."

Kentucky. No wonder Nana was glad to have my father out of the way. She'd never welcome a hillbilly Kentuckian as a son-in-law. Granted, outsiders sometimes viewed Brown County as hillbilly country, but Nana held her beloved hometown far above that. She was enormously proud of Nashville's rustic, tourist-attracting charm, but in her eyes, all the other villages in the sparsely-populated county—Spearsville, Fruitdale, Bean Blossom, Helmsburg, Trevlac, Needmore, Gnawbone—counted for nothing. "Hick towns," she called them.

However, Nana did deign to attend St. Augustine's Episcopal Church in the neighboring village of Bean Blossom, where she served on the vestry. For over thirty years, my mother and I sat in the pew on either side of her, like her personal accoutrements. Every Sunday, our priest shook each of our hands in turn, and he praised our example of close family ties more times than I can count.

CHAPTER 3

I don't believe Nana ever held high hopes that I'd turn out to be anything special. And seeing my mediocrity reflected in her critical eyes taught me to expect little of myself.

In spite of the fact that every school night found me diligently completing homework assignments at Nana's dining room table, I never succeeded in joining the ranks of the excellent students.

When I entered junior high, Nana suggested that I sign up for band, and before I knew it, she'd bought me a clarinet.

"A clarinet!" I protested. "I wanted a trombone."

"Don't be silly, Elaine," she snapped.

But my short stint with band class quickly proved that I had no aptitude with a musical instrument, and Nana promptly sold my barely used clarinet to the parents of a girl who showed more promise.

During my freshman year of high school, Nana pushed me to try out for cheerleading. "You need to put yourself out there, Elaine. I can tell you've settled for being a wallflower, and I don't like that."

But my feeble jumps and breathless cheers failed to impress the cheerleading sponsor, who didn't give me a second glance. I was cut during the first round of tryouts, along with all the other clumsy, mousy girls who'd dared to dream of popularity.

"Well, I suppose you're not athletic enough," Nana conceded. "What are we going to do with you, Elaine?"

The only positive comment Nana ever made about my abilities was that I had artistic inclinations. My sketches and watercolor paintings of our native wooded hills were the only things I did that put a smile on her face. "If you really buckle down and apply yourself, Elaine," she told me, "your work might eventually be good enough to display in the Brown County Art Gallery."

Nana liked to think of herself as culturally sophisticated, and was proud of the fact that she was on a first-name basis with most of the local artists. Having a granddaughter numbered in their ranks would have been a dollop of delectable icing on the big fat cake of her life among Nashville's elite. So from early adolescence, I was steered in the direction of majoring in art at Indiana University in Bloomington.

When the time came for me to head off to college, I talked to my mother and Nana about living in a dorm on the IU campus. But the idea scared me more than it excited me, and I was secretly relieved when Nana said, "Elaine, I don't think you're mature enough for that."

So I ended up commuting the nineteen miles between my home and Bloomington, in the two-year-old Toyota Nana bought me as a high school graduation gift.

Life as an art major wasn't anything like my fantasies, or Nana's, for that matter. University art classes had nothing to do with the old barns, covered bridges, and autumn splendors of her artist friends. I discovered that I wasn't nearly as talented or creative as my classmates, and their unorthodox ideas intimidated me. When a B-minus proved to be the highest grade I ever managed to earn on an assignment, I became despondent.

Midway through the second semester, I was faced with the task of sketching a nude male model in the classroom. I hadn't had much experience with the male body, as I'd barely even dated in high school. I'd never seen the nether regions of a living, breathing man, but that day, there they were, right in my line of vision. I was so unnerved that my drawing deteriorated into a disorganized mess, and when my ill-tempered instructor looked over my shoulder and barked out critical comments, I knew I couldn't take anymore humiliation.

I didn't usually break down in front of Nana, but that evening, I sat at the dining room table and sobbed. She stood over me, hands on her hips, slowly shaking her big blonde head as if disgusted by my display of weakness.

"I can't go back, Nana," I choked out. "I'm not good enough."

"What are you talking about, Elaine?" she demanded to know.

"I'm dropping out of school."

"Don't you think you need to pull yourself together and give it another try?"

"I've already tried, Nana. I've tried so many times. I just can't do it."

"Okay, then," she huffed, turning away from me. "I didn't think I raised a quitter, but if you don't believe you can make it in the art program, then you might as well drop out now."

I knew she'd already figured out that, as an art student, I was a hopeless case. I knew that was why she didn't push me harder.

As she was about to leave the room, she turned back and said, "But you're going to have to find something else to do, Elaine."

The cold finality in her voice chilled me. It felt like she was washing her hands of me, and I realized this was the same heartless attitude my mother had faced when she went against Nana and married my father. If you thwarted Nana's will, you were on your own.

I moped around the house for three weeks, thinking about what I wanted to do with my life. I'd never before had to face this difficult question, as up to that point, I'd done nothing but follow the path Nana had paved for me.

"What are you good at, Elaine?" I whispered over and over to myself. In moments of self-loathing, I answered with, "Nothing. You're good for nothing."

Still, I tried to come up with options that could save me from heading down the fast track to Loser-ville. I even tried making a written inventory of my skills.

One evening when I was holed up in my bedroom contemplating my pitiful list, I heard Nana calling me.

"Why don't you come out here in the land of the living, Elaine?" Her voice sounded weirdly lighthearted, and I wondered if she was trying to make up for her earlier harshness.

When I stepped into the living room, she flashed me a sickeningly sweet smile, and then sighed with exaggerated weariness. "I've been on my feet all day, Elaine. They sure could use a good massage."

Her request revolted me, and for a moment, I was conscious of how much I hated her. Nevertheless, I ignored the anger churning in the pit of my stomach and did what I'd done a hundred times before. Like a dutiful servant, I sat down on the ottoman in front of the queen's chair and took one of her fat feet into my lap. As my fingers expertly massaged, probing into the sore spots I knew all too well, Nana groaned with pleasure.

"I don't know how you do this, Elaine," she said. "I think you're better at this than my own massage therapist."

Suddenly, something changed in the room. I can't describe it exactly, but the atmosphere felt different, like someone or something else had joined the two of us. I continued to watch my strong, square hands moving expertly over Nana's fleshy foot, and it seemed like they were lit up and glowing. Then a thought came to me, clear as a bell: *Why, of course, Elaine, this is what you'll do professionally.*

I've thought about that surreal moment many times since then. I've wondered whether Nana set the whole thing up to help me out after my failure with art school, to give me a nudge in another direction. When I think about it that way, it seems a little creepy. I prefer to think Nana had nothing to do with my epiphany, that she was just a pawn in the beautifully orchestrated plan of some higher power.

Wherever my inspiration came from, it left me knowing exactly what I needed to do next. Instead of heading my Toyota west toward Bloomington's IU campus, I embarked upon a twice-weekly northbound commute to a massage therapy training program in Indianapolis.

A year later, when I presented my certificate to Nana, she said, "Good for you, Elaine. I knew you could do it."

Evidently, she didn't think I could manage anything else on my own, as once again, she took matters into her own hands. She convinced her chiropractor to lease me a treatment room in his office, and surprisingly, he sent a steady stream of referrals my way. Before I knew it, I'd built a thriving practice.

I've often wondered whether Nana slipped her chiropractor something under the table to get those referrals started. I really don't think so. Her influence was strong enough that she didn't need to resort to bribery.

Maybe I don't give myself enough credit. It's entirely possible that I was good enough to earn those referrals on my own.

CHAPTER 4

Five years into my massage practice, Kevin Hickman limped into my treatment room, having injured his knee in a pick-up basketball game. I'd attended Brown County High School with Kevin, but I didn't recognize him at first, as his trademark mop of curly blonde hair had thinned and his skinny adolescent build had thickened. Still, he was a nice-looking, affable man, and I enjoyed talking with him.

During high school, I'd had a crush on Kevin that lasted about three weeks. He'd taken me to the senior prom, but had never called me after that. I'd chalked it up to the fact that I'd worn the puffy yellow dress Nana had bought me at a time when the other girls were wearing black and slinky, and figured he'd been embarrassed to be seen with me. After a few tears of humiliation, I'd focused my youthful infatuation on someone else.

I was surprised to learn that Kevin had also attended Indiana University, as I'd never seen him on campus. However, he'd stuck around long enough to graduate, and had returned to our former high school to teach chemistry.

I worked on Kevin's knee twice a week for six weeks, and at the end of that time, he told me it felt good as new. "I'm pretty sure you saved me from having surgery, Elaine," he said. "Let me thank you by taking you out to dinner." So we shared a pleasant meal of country-fried chicken and hot fried biscuits at the Nashville House restaurant.

I didn't expect to hear from Kevin again, but he called me a few days later, and after six months of half-hearted dating, we decided to get married. I'm not sure why. Maybe it was because neither of us had any other prospects, and we agreed to settle for each other.

I don't think Nana was overly impressed with Kevin, but she didn't object to him and seemed to think he was good enough for someone like me. For three months, her life revolved around planning my flamboyant wedding, which was held at St. Augustine's. Sadly, the most vivid memory I have of my wedding day is that my mind wandered during the ceremony, as if the event wasn't all that important.

As a wedding gift, Nana gave Kevin and me enough money for the down-payment on a home. We bought a small, two-story log house on State Road 135, halfway between Bean Blossom and Nashville. The house was set back off the road on a wooded lot, and a long, winding gravel lane led to our unattached garage. The downstairs of the house consisted of a kitchen, living room, bedroom, and bathroom. The upstairs, with its slanted ceiling, contained the second bedroom.

Our living quarters were rather cramped, but adequate for two people. The place was a bit rundown, not nearly as nice as Nana's home on Artist Drive, and Kevin wasn't exactly handy with repairs. But it was a space I could call my own, and I loved every inch of it.

Although my marriage didn't last, I really can't complain about it. Six months into the marriage, I knew I wasn't in love with Kevin, and that I never had been. Still, I wasn't unhappy. Kevin was easygoing and non-demanding, and I loved the personal freedom he allowed me. Even though I never mustered the courage to venture into the realm of the outrageous, I enjoyed decorating our home as I pleased, dressing as I pleased, coming and going as I pleased, all without fear of criticism. While there were no fireworks in our relationship, there was no drama, no jealousy, no mind-games, and Kevin and I got along well as housemates.

We shared some good times, attending athletic events at the high school or shows at the Brown County Playhouse. Occasionally, we drove to Bloomington to watch movies at the Indiana University Cinema. In the summer, Kevin played softball at Deer Run Park, just outside of Nashville. He was considered to be the best pitcher in his league, and I sat in the bleachers and pretended to be thrilled by my husband's star performance.

We managed to get along with each other's families. Kevin's three older brothers had long been married, so having a daughter-in-law was no novelty for his parents. They took little interest in me, and I neither liked nor disliked them. And no matter how many barbs Nana hurled his way, they never seemed to snag Kevin's thick skin.

I don't believe I ever would have made a move to end my marriage. But after three years, Kevin told me he was filing for divorce, on the grounds that there was no chemistry between us.

Even though this devastating news left me reeling with shock, it struck me as funny that chemistry was so important to my husband, both at work and at home. I soon learned that he was using his no-chemistry excuse to justify his affair with the young student teacher assigned to his classroom, the bubbly Jessica of the tight tops and deep cleavage.

After our divorce, I took back my maiden name of Greene. Not that I was eager to embrace my old identity. But I knew my failed marriage gave Nana another reason to look down her nose at me, and I didn't want the *Hick* portion of the Hickman name reminding me of my inferior status on a daily basis.

Kevin told me he'd be the one to move out the house, as he had no right to claim something my grandmother had put so much money into. That was decent of him. Nana suggested that I sell the house and move back home.

"If you stay there, you'll be living hand-to-mouth on just your income," she told me. "There's no point in that."

But I'd had a taste of freedom, and I stood my ground. Even though I knew my budget would be tight, I was determined to find a way to keep the home I'd grown to love. So I moved my bedroom furniture into the unused upstairs room. Then I terminated the lease on my space at the chiropractor's office and moved my massage practice into the downstairs bedroom.

I told myself that implementing this money-saving strategy was the sensible thing to do. But deep down, I knew my divorce had shaken my confidence, and that I was withdrawing from the world into the refuge of my home.

When my last client would leave at the end of my work day, the house would seem deadly quiet. After a year of such solitude, I told myself I needed something else in my home that lived and breathed.

So one hot June day, I drove down to the Brown County Humane Society in Gnawbone with fifty dollars in hand, intent on adopting a feline companion. I walked back and forth in front of the cat cages, trying to decide between the orange tabby and the black-and-white tuxedo cat with the little mustache.

Maybe I'll just get both, I thought. I hadn't brought enough cash to adopt two animals. Just as I turned to ask the shelter worker if they took credit cards, a bolt of fear shot through me, riveting my feet to the concrete floor. And the accompanying thought screamed, *YOU'RE TOO YOUNG TO TURN INTO THE SPINSTER CAT-LADY!*

"So have you decided?" the shelter worker asked me.

"Not yet," I mumbled. "I'll have to think about it." Then I turned and ran from the building.

When I got home, I brought in my mail and tossed it on the table. There on the top of the stack was a flyer advertising ballroom dance lessons at Buck's Dance Hall. "Singles and couples welcome," it said. The cost was fifty dollars for a series of ten classes.

I looked at the fifty-dollar-bill I was still clutching in my sweaty hand, the designated cat money, and it seemed like a sign to me. Before I could talk myself out of the idea, I picked up the phone and registered for the class, and two weeks later, I presented the same fifty-dollar-bill at the Dance Hall's check-in table.

CHAPTER 5

I was so afraid of being late for the class that I ended up arriving at Buck's Dance Hall way too early. When I entered the building, the only other person there was the woman at the check-in table.

"Am I . . . am I at the right place for the ballroom dance lessons?" I stammered, looking around the empty hall.

"Yes, you are," she said. "We've registered a full class. The others will be here soon."

She handed me a stick-on nametag, on which I wrote *Elaine Greene* in black Magic Marker. Then she pointed me to the row of chairs around the periphery of the large floor, and I took a seat in the corner farthest away from the door.

I sat there, feeling like an idiot, for a full five minutes before anyone else showed up. Then the other students started drifting in. Most of them were well-dressed couples much older than me. I felt self-conscious in my drab outfit, a knee-length denim skirt, a pale yellow top, and scuffed black loafers.

I saw my high school English teacher, but as she glanced around the room, her eyes swept right past me. My invisibility depressed me, and I berated myself for coming to a place where I didn't belong. However, a few minutes later, a man I knew from St. Augustine's smiled and nodded at me. One of my massage clients lifted a hand in greeting while moving on to talk with someone else.

I was glad when I saw two women walk in together. At least I wouldn't stand out as the only single person in the class.

And then I forgot all about being nervous, because the next couple who came through the door captured my full attention. My first fleeting impression was that they were a homosexual couple.

Not that the shorter of the two men looked gay. He was an unremarkable guy, balding and slouchy, wearing a goofy grin. The tail of his rumpled shirt was coming un-tucked from the trousers sagging off his skinny bottom.

It was his partner who held my attention, a 5'11", 230 pound drag-queen with a strong, masculine jaw-line and jutting chin. The large, round, heavy-lidded eyes behind his wire-rimmed glasses reminded me of a sleepy owl. He wore a platinum blonde shoulder-length wig, bright red lipstick, red pumps, and a dress that was the height of fashion ten years earlier.

A moment later, I realized that the drag-queen's ample bosom actually belonged to a very homely fifty-year-old woman. And when she and her partner meandered in my direction, I saw that her stick-on nametag bore the name *Suzette Perry* rendered in perfect calligraphy.

Suzette Perry. The names on everyone else's stick-on tags blurred together in my mind, but hers remained clearly etched in my memory.

Thankfully, I discovered that I was no more inept than any of the other students in mastering beginning steps in the waltz, foxtrot, and swing. And neither was Suzette Perry. In fact, she showed more aptitude than most of the others.

The dance teacher had us constantly changing partners, as a way of working the single people into the rotation. When it was my turn to sit out, I found myself following Suzette's every move. I was inexplicably mesmerized by her, finding her simultaneously ungainly and graceful, cheaply gaudy yet regal. While she wasn't the drag-queen I'd first thought her to be, she certainly carried herself like the queen of some realm. When she executed an elegant twirl under her partner's raised arm, her skirt flared out, exposing long, shapely legs that contrasted with the boxy bulk of her upper body.

Our dance teacher was an instructor from Arthur Murray's in Bloomington. I figured he'd agreed to teach a beginner's level at the Dance Hall as a way of luring students into his studio for more advanced lessons. We were awed by his superb talent, and addressed him formally as *Mr. Cassidy.*

All of us except for Suzette Perry. "Hey," she called out while he was demonstrating a step in the foxtrot. "That's not the way you showed us last time."

He looked startled. "Yes, it is. I always teach it this way."

"No," Suzette insisted. "You said it was this way." She dropped her partner's hand and stepped out in front of Mr. Cassidy, then daintily executed her own version of the footwork.

She proceeded to hold up the class for a full ten minutes, arguing with Mr. Cassidy, then demanding that he demonstrate the step over and over until she was sure she understood it.

The rest of the class stood back, watching silently. I wondered what these sensible people thought of the weird, outspoken, owl-eyed Suzette. Suddenly, I felt sorry for her. I wanted to smack the smirks off their smug faces, to tell them they had no right to judge her.

But Suzette apparently wasn't concerned about what the other students thought of her. She seemed fully confident in exercising her right to ask questions and speak her opinion.

When Mr. Cassidy announced it was time for a fifteen-minute break, the thought of milling around with the other students made me extremely nervous. So I scurried over to my chair in the corner and rooted around in my handbag for the paperback novel I'd brought with me.

But then I looked up and saw Suzette Perry walking toward me. Terror grabbed my insides. It was one thing to watch this unusual woman from a safe distance, but I had no idea how to deal with her on a personal basis.

She seated herself in the chair next to mine. Turning her heavy body toward me, she crossed one long leg over the other, her size-eleven red pump extending out in front of us, her large hands folded elegantly on her lap. I noticed how long her fingers were. The nails were perfectly shaped and painted light pink, with tiny flowers etched on the tips.

"You're so cute," she said, sighing dramatically. "All these horny old dudes can't wait for their turn to get their hands on you."

I stared at her, flabbergasted.

"They surely don't want any of this." She gestured toward herself with a flutter of her hand.

I had no idea how to respond to her outrageous social overture. She grinned, apparently sensing my discomfort. I noticed that one of her top teeth, the third from the front, was missing. It made her smile seem childlike.

"You're really quiet," she said. "You need to mingle more, open up a little bit. You can start by talking with me. I'm Suzette Perry."

Suddenly, I felt like I couldn't breathe. I had no room to back away or to put up a mental barrier like I usually did in uncomfortable social situations. It felt like Suzette Perry had enveloped me in her aura, taking possession of me, and there

I was, defenseless in her clutches.

My downcast eyes flickered up to meet hers, and I saw compassion in her gaze. I realized that the woman I'd pitied twenty minutes earlier now felt sorry for me, the socially awkward shy girl.

"I'm Elaine Greene," I said.

"Do they call you Lanie?" she asked. "You look like a Lanie."

"No, everyone calls me Elaine."

"Well, I'm going to call you Lanie. You'll be Lanie to me."

CHAPTER 6

Over the next nine weeks of class, Suzette graced me with her larger-than-life presence at every break. Each time she'd seat herself in the chair next to mine, I'd have a moment of breathlessness, a feeling of suffocation. Then I'd relax and settle into our interchange.

Like a talk-show host, she interviewed me artfully, capturing me in her owlish gaze. I had difficulty responding to her queries with more than a few words, but she'd ask more questions if she wasn't satisfied with what I offered. As she gleaned bits of my personal information, she regaled me with details of her own life.

"Where do you live, Lanie?" she asked the second week.

"Nashville," I responded. "Actually, on State Road 135 between Bean Blossom and Nashville, but it's closer to Nashville."

"Oh," she said. "Eldon and I must've driven past your place on our way here. We'll have to stop by sometime."

I cringed at the thought of her knocking on my front door, hapless husband in tow. Nevertheless, I responded with politeness. "Where do you live?"

"Helmsburg," she said, grinning proudly. "I'm originally from Morgantown, but when I married Eldon, we bought a little place in the country, just west of Helmsburg on Lick Creek Road. I love it there."

Helmsburg! My mind flashed back to my years at Nashville Elementary School, when we students would climb into a bus and travel the eight miles to Helmsburg Elementary for a ballgame or a spelling bee. Whatever the competition, we Nashville kids would invariably win, and on the way back to our own school, we'd wallow in our superiority, scoffing at the Helmsburg nitwits, calling them names.

At that moment, I felt so ashamed of my younger self that if I'd been Catholic instead of Episcopalian, I would have rushed to the priest for confession.

"So, are you married?" Suzette asked, interrupting my guilty reverie.

"No," I replied, "I'm divorced."

"How many times have you been married?"

"Just once."

"Of course, you're just a kid. You're not old enough to have been married more than once. How old are you, anyway?"

"I'm thirty."

"Oh, you've got plenty of time to get married again. I've been married and divorced three times. Eldon's my fourth husband. Don't give up hope, Lanie. Sometimes it takes awhile to find the right guy."

She gestured toward her slouchy partner, who at that very moment was in the process of giving one of his female classmates a hug. I'd already noticed Eldon's habit of greeting women with lingering embraces. The younger and prettier they were, the more likely they were to be recipients of his unwelcome attention. The women in the class had learned to avert their gaze when they saw him coming, so as not to encourage him.

Suzette rolled her eyes. "Oh God, the old goat's at it again. Don't worry, Lanie, he's harmless."

I bit the inside of my cheek to keep from laughing. I couldn't picture creepy old Eldon Perry as any woman's right guy.

The next week, Suzette asked, "What do you do for a living?"

"I'm a massage therapist," I replied. "I work out of my home."

"Oh, that's interesting!" she chortled. "I love getting massages. They help the pain in my legs and feet from my diabetes. Maybe I can get one from you sometime."

"Maybe you can," I said, once again cringing inwardly.

"Did you have to go to college to be a massage therapist?"

I hesitated before phrasing my response. "I did go to college, but not for massage therapy. I dropped out, and then went to massage therapy school."

"I never got the chance to go to college," Suzette said sadly. "I wish I could've. What did you study when you were in college?"

"I was an art major."

She grinned from ear to ear, showing her missing tooth. "That's so exciting! We have so much in common! I love art. I have a craft business in my home. You'll have to come over some time and see what I do."

The following week, I learned that in no aspect of her life, past or present, was this would-be friend of mine legally *Suzette*. She was born Virginia Sue Harding, the youngest child and only girl in a large family of boys. Her father, the minister of a small church in Morgantown, was evidently too busy tending his flock to notice what was going on in his own family, leaving her brothers free to torment her.

"My mother was the only one in the family who treated me decently," Suzette confided tearfully. "But she died when I was twelve. My father wasn't any better than my brothers. The son-of-a-bitch died ten years ago."

Over the weeks, Suzette's eyes often welled with tears as she told me stories of abuse that had inflicted emotional wounds that never healed. I sat there, a captive audience of one, desperately not wanting to hear these sad tales, but I couldn't bring myself to do anything that would make this vulnerable woman feel rejected.

Once when her tears spilled over and ran down her cheeks, I rummaged through my bag and handed her a tissue.

"Thanks, Lanie," she sniffled. I could see that my gesture touched her deeply, and I knew she believed a bond was growing between the two of us. Strangely, I felt it, too.

After drying her tears, Suzette told me that at seventeen, she decided she'd had her fill of abuse, and she ran away from home and went to California with her boyfriend. The minute they landed on California soil, she shed the identity of *Virginia*, as she considered the name to be too old-fashioned. For awhile, she used her middle name, but then decided that *Sue* was too plain and opted to embellish it.

During her twenty-four years in California, she lived through one calamity after another, marrying and divorcing three husbands. "I never had children," she told me. "I wasn't able to. I was upset about that for awhile, but now I'm glad. This world can be a rotten place, and I wouldn't want to be responsible for bringing another human being into this mess."

Suzette's third divorce left her destitute, so she returned to her home community where she married Eldon Perry. Eldon supported her with his accountant's income, allowing her the luxury of staying home and working with her crafts.

The last week of class, Suzette captured me in her gaze, and then contorted her homely face into a childish pout.

"Lanie, I'm afraid I'll never see you again."

While I searched my mind for a reassuring but noncommittal response, she said, "Eldon and I are having a party at our house next Saturday. It's our tenth wedding anniversary. I want you to come."

As I opened my mouth to utter a *maybe,* she said, "No, you're coming. I'm not letting you crawl back into your little shell. You're coming, and that's that."

"Okay," I said meekly.

CHAPTER 7

I'd never been a party person, and everything in me protested against the idea of going to Suzette's anniversary celebration. But I'd given her my word, and I knew I couldn't live with myself if I let her down.

So on a warm Saturday evening in September, I drove north on State Road 135 to Bean Blossom. Then I turned west on State Road 45, passing cornfields and patches of woods as I traveled the hilly, winding road. After crossing the railroad tracks, I made a left turn and drove parallel to the tracks on down into the small town of Helmsburg.

Just on the other side of Helmsburg, I turned north onto Lick Creek Road. Following Suzette's list of landmarks, I passed a few homes perched high on tree-covered hills. Shortly after crossing the creek, I spotted Suzette's drive on the left-hand side of the road, leading up the hill to her two-story, wood-sided residence.

As I eased my car up the steep driveway, I could see that the Perrys' home had once been an attractive dwelling. Now, it looked as if Eldon and Suzette were unable to stay on top of property maintenance.

The paint on the blue siding and the white window trim was cracked and peeling, giving the home a bedraggled appearance. Scraggly cedar shrubs grew on one side of the front door. The shrubs on the other side had been dug up and were lying in the yard, along with an overturned wheelbarrow. It looked as if someone had lost interest in the middle of a landscaping project.

The small yard, surrounded by woods, had been recently mowed but not trimmed, and tall, spiky grass encircled the trees, the overturned wheelbarrow, and an old birdbath. A flowerbed bordered with river rocks contained a few dried-up marigolds and many thriving weeds.

Three cars were parked in the driveway at the top of the hill, and a few more on the edge of the yard. I carefully pulled alongside a hastily parked pickup truck that had gouged furrows in the lawn. Then I got out of my car and climbed the Perrys' crumbling brick steps, my stomach churning at the prospect of facing a houseful of people I didn't know.

My knock on the door triggered the frantic barking of a small dog in the house. "Shut up, Daisy!" I heard Suzette scream.

Then Eldon opened the door, greeting me with a goofy grin. "Come on in, Lanie," he said, gathering me in his arms for his trademark lingering hug.

When I finally extricated myself from Eldon's embrace, I stepped into the crowd of alcohol-buzzed party guests. Suzette waved from across the room as she tried to contain an overly excited Chihuahua on her lap.

"Hi, Lanie," she called. Then she bellowed to her noisy guests, "Hey! Everybody shut up and listen! This is my friend Lanie Greene."

The unkempt people milling around the room, lounging on the shabby furniture, and sprawling across the scuffed hardwood floor were all complete strangers to me. None of them gave me more than a disinterested glance.

What the heck am I doing here? I wondered. *Why am I hanging out with these scuzzy people?*

Then I recognized Arlene Greene's bigoted voice in my own head, and I felt ashamed. I decided I'd do whatever I could to make the best of the next few hours.

As I glanced around the living room, I saw that every inch

of wall and shelf space was crammed full of samples of Suzette's craft projects, items rendered in resin, ceramic, and wood. To still my nerves, I wandered around examining her handiwork.

Wow! I thought. *She's really good at what she does!* Somehow, I'd expected her work to be amateurish.

I edged into the adjacent, less-crowded dining room to see what treasures it held. Suddenly, Suzette was at my side. "Wanna drink, Lanie?" she asked.

Thinking I'd better keep my wits in this unfamiliar environment, I said, "No, thanks."

"How about a soft drink?" she persisted. She held up the glass she was carrying. "I have to stick to diet Coke myself, because of my diabetes. Want a diet Coke?"

"Sure."

I picked up a ceramic figurine of a whimsical cherub, and as I studied its intricate details, Suzette returned with my drink.

"Lanie, do you sculpt?"

"I did a little bit in my high school art class," I said. "But that was a long time ago."

Suzette held up an index finger. "Hang on just a minute."

She left the room again, and when she returned a few moments later, she tossed me a ball of clay. "Sit here at the table and sculpt me something," she commanded. "Make me a bunny rabbit."

Several of her guests came over to see what we were doing. I panicked at the thought of disappointing Suzette, especially in front of an audience. Nevertheless, I sat down at the table and began squeezing the clay, warming it in my hands.

Suzette sat down next to me, and I could feel her watching

every movement of my fingers. The rabbit began to take shape as I formed its long ears, a rounded back, and a little puff tail.

"Wow, you're good!" one female onlooker exclaimed.

"Pretty cool," her male companion commented.

I placed the sculpted bunny into Suzette's outstretched palm. She beamed at me as if I was Heaven-sent.

"Lanie, I had a feeling about you," she said, her voice thick with emotion. "Somehow, I knew you'd be the one. I can make molds, but I can't sculpt worth anything. I've been praying to find a sculptor I can work with, and here you are."

I stared at her, dumfounded.

Suzette stood up and selected several figurines from her hutch, then brought them back to the table. Handing me a chubby Santa, she said, "This one's in resin. I made the rubber mold for it."

Then she showed me an angel with folded hands. "This is ceramic. The molding process for this piece is completely different. I make both kinds of molds. All I need is someone to do the sculpting. Then there will be no end to what I can do."

As she babbled on about the work we could do together, I felt as if my head was spinning in circles. I was being pulled into something I didn't understand, something I hadn't consented to. I wanted to protest, to back off, but once again, I felt powerless to do so.

"I can take our things to craft fairs in Bloomington and Indianapolis," Suzette continued. "There's a shop in Nashville that would probably sell them. We could even sell things on the internet. Eldon could create a website for us." She looked up at her husband, who'd joined the crowd of observers. "Couldn't you, sweetie?"

He nodded, grinning.

Never in my life have I been as confused as I was sitting there at Suzette's dining room table, surrounded by admiring onlookers. I'd thought my short stint as an art student had proven to the world my utter worthlessness as an artist, yet there I sat, heralded as a divine gift bestowed upon Suzette, the long-awaited sculptor she'd been praying for.

"So . . . what . . . what do you want me to start on?" I stammered.

"I'm going to a craft show in Greenwood next month," she said. "I want to make some old-fashioned pull toys with farm animals on them. How about if you make me a cow and a pig?" She clapped her hands, grinning from ear to ear. "I'm so excited!"

Before I left her party, Suzette loaded me down with clay and sculpting tools, along with the specifications for my first sculpting project.

CHAPTER 8

I didn't have enough confidence in my knowledge of cow and pig anatomy to sculpt those creatures without the use of visual aids. So Sunday afternoon, the day after Suzette's party, I drove to a farm along Spearsville Road, where I stopped to photograph cows grazing in the pasture.

I realized there weren't many pig farmers in Brown County, but I did know of one family near Bean Blossom that kept a single pig in a small field near their house. Photographing the uncooperative pig proved to be more difficult than dealing with placid cows, and passers-by gave me funny looks when they saw me straining to snap shots with my digital camera from every possible angle.

A pickup truck slowed down, catching me leaning precariously over the fence. "You like that hog, honey?" the driver shouted through his open window. "Careful, you're gonna fall in there with him."

Embarrassed, I told myself it was time to quit. I went home, downloaded and printed the best of my photos, and spread them out on the kitchen table to use as guides for my sculpting.

The rest of the week, I forgot all about being lonely in my home, because I was so engrossed in Suzette's assignment. Each evening after my last massage client left for the day, I worked on my animal sculptures. I was surprised at how much I enjoyed the art form, and my imagination raced ahead of me, suggesting all kinds of brilliant possibilities for my sculpting future.

The following Saturday morning, I packed my precious cow and pig figurines in a shoebox, tucking tissue paper around them to keep them from getting jostled on the drive to Suzette's house.

Once again, my knock on the Perrys' front door elicited excited canine barking, followed by Suzette screaming, "Shut up, Daisy!" She opened the door wearing a cotton housecoat and a pair of ugly brown slippers, which I assumed belonged to her husband. Gone was the blonde wig she'd worn to the dance class and the anniversary party, and I saw that her natural hair was wispy, gray, and in need of a fresh perm.

"Damn dog," she muttered. "Come on in, Lanie."

As she led me through the living room, I noticed that the house was still cluttered with signs of last weekend's party. Beer cans, paper plates, plastic forks, and crumpled napkins lay on the coffee table, the fireplace mantle, and the sofa. The hardwood floor, littered with dog hair and broken potato chips, clearly hadn't been swept in some time.

"Excuse this dump," she said. "Excuse how I look. It's just one of those days." Gesturing toward her slippers, she added, "Some days, I can't wear shoes because the neuropathy in my feet flares up and kicks my ass."

She took the shoebox from my hand, and then motioned for me to have a seat at the dining room table. Breathing heavily, she lowered her body into the chair across from mine.

Ever so carefully, she removed my pieces from their tissue-paper bed. Then, head tilted back, she looked down her nose through her bifocals as she turned the figures over in her graceful, man-sized hands, her long, pink-nailed fingers moving delicately over my work.

I found myself keeping rhythm with her labored breathing as I waited for her verdict on my creations.

"These are really nice, Lanie," she finally said. "I like them a lot. But you might as well know I'm going to be blunt with you when something isn't right, and I don't want you to get hurt feelings."

She held out the figure of the cow. "See these undercuts around the ears and the nostrils? That's not going to work. I won't be able to get it out of the mold without breaking it. You did the same thing with the pig."

I stared down at the table, feeling chastened and deflated. "I'm sorry."

"It's okay," Suzette said, her stern voice softening. "You'll learn. I have all the confidence in the world in you, Lanie. You can fix your mistakes right now. Let's go downstairs to my studio."

She led me to a door off her kitchen, and I followed her down a steep, narrow, cobweb-strewn staircase, feeling like I was about to enter a vampire's underground lair or a mad scientist's secret laboratory. Our descent into the unknown seemed interminable, as Suzette's slippered feet searched painfully for each step, her palms pressing against the dank walls for support.

Suddenly, the narrow staircase opened into a room that looked as if it had been hit by gale-force winds. Rubber and ceramic molds lay on tables, shelves, windowsills, and chairs. Unpainted figurines stood here and there among the rubble, some of them broken or misshapen. Bottles of acrylic paint sat in random clusters around the room, along with handfuls of brushes stuffed into aluminum cans. Wooden pieces in various stages of the painting process lay on every available surface.

Muttering to herself, Suzette poked around in the wreckage, pushing aside a broken mold, righting a figurine that had toppled over. "I've been trying to get Eldon to come down here and help me clean up this mess. But he just stays upstairs sleeping in his chair."

Finally, she came up with a lump of clay and several sculpting tools, and I cleared a small space on one of the tables. As I worked on correcting my errors on the cow and pig figurines, Suzette sat on the other side of the table, watching me.

I found her restlessness, her deep sighs, and her labored breathing to be disconcerting, and after a few minutes, I blurted out, "Are you okay, Suzette?"

"Oh, it's nothing," she said. "My blood sugar's high, that's all. When I took it this morning, it was over 300."

"Shouldn't you do something?" I asked, alarmed.

"I already gave myself a shot of insulin. I'll be okay. My sugar always runs high. I never get it under 200."

I grimaced. "Yikes! That doesn't sound good."

Suzette laughed bitterly. "Lanie, I'm a fifty-two-year-old woman living in an eighty-year-old body. I'm falling apart, but I've gotten used to the idea. The diabetes is just the tip of the iceberg. I've got high blood pressure, and now my doctor's saying I have congestive heart failure. Isn't that just dandy? It sucks, but that's the way it is."

"I'm so sorry," I said.

She waved her hand dismissively. "I guess when my time's up, it's up, and there's nothing I can do about it."

I tried to imagine what it would be like to face life with her physical challenges. A wave of sadness washed over me. I wanted to offer something hopeful. As I searched for words, Suzette broke the awkward silence between us.

"Will you be taking any more lessons at Buck's Dance Hall?"

"I don't know," I said. "I haven't thought about it. How about you?"

"Nope. Eldon and I won't be going back."

"Why not? You enjoyed it so much."

She sighed. "I did. I loved it. Ballroom dancing is so romantic. But it was too hard on my legs and feet. The day after every class, I'd hurt so bad I couldn't stand it. I couldn't even get out of bed. Nope, my dancing days are over."

I glanced up from my work and saw a tear trickle from one of her heavy-lidded eyes. She reached up and brushed it away with the back of her elegant, pink-nailed hand.

CHAPTER 9

I was soon glad I hadn't backed out of Suzette's plans for working together. I can't say we ever produced anything brilliant, and I received only a handful of dollars for my share of the profit from sales at her craft shows. However, the time we spent together working on our joint creations pulled us close into a bond of friendship.

Throughout the first fall and winter of our partnership, I drove to Helmsburg two or three times a month to deliver whatever sculptures Suzette had assigned me to do: animals, fairy-tale characters, holiday figurines. Then I'd take home supplies and instructions for the next project.

Now and then, I'd spend a Saturday afternoon in her basement studio, helping her get ready for a craft show. It took me awhile to get past my aversion to the clutter. But Suzette reigned like a queen in the middle of her mess, quite able to find everything she needed.

She'd allow me to paint the basecoat on figures, but reserved the fine detail work and the dry-brushing for herself. She'd growl at me to clean my paintbrushes properly. "They're expensive, you know."

Suzette was seldom quiet, and while we worked, she regaled me with stories about her life in California. "My first husband Bob beat me, that son-of-a-bitch," she told me. She pointed to the space where her tooth was missing. "He did this." Then she detailed other injuries he'd inflicted on her, and the numerous trips she'd made to the emergency room.

"I finally got to the point where I'd taken all I was going to take from that man," she said. "One day when I saw him coming at me, I prayed, 'Lord, help me.' All of a sudden, I felt a rush of adrenalin. I picked up a kitchen chair and clobbered him with it. I beat that stupid jerk with the chair until he begged for mercy." She grinned. "Then I hit him a few more times. He learned his lesson. He never touched me again."

I put down my paintbrush and applauded. "Good for you!"

Suzette shrugged. "I give God the credit for that adrenalin surge. I couldn't have done it on my own. Sometimes, He answers prayer in ways you wouldn't expect."

We sat in silence for awhile, contemplating the mysteries of divine intervention. Then Suzette resumed her storytelling.

"My second husband Carl was a real charmer. I adored that man. God, was he ever good in bed!" She shook her head, grinning lasciviously. "He was so sweet and attentive. He had wonderful, gentle hands, and I loved the way he touched me. After my first husband, I thought Carl was God's gift to me."

Her face darkened, and I waited for the inevitable cruel twist in her story. "Carl's only fault was that he couldn't stick to one woman. I knew he was having affairs, but I tried to convince myself I could handle that. Then he got my best friend pregnant. She didn't want the baby, and Carl had the nerve to ask me if I'd help him raise it."

I stared at her, wide-eyed. "Unbelievable!"

"I know," she said. "Can you imagine? I told him, 'No friggin' way!' He got mad and walked out on me.

"My third husband Tim was a flat-out loser. I don't know what I was doing when I married him. I guess I was too shook up over Carl. Couldn't think straight. Tim had a drug problem and ended up running us deep into debt. I had nothing to live on, nowhere to go, so I came back home."

In spite of the hair-raising details of Suzette's stories, there was something about working in that messy studio and listening to the sound of her voice that lulled me into a state of deep relaxation. The hours would pass quickly, and I'd be reluctant to leave.

I became increasingly aware that, in spite of her gruffness, Suzette had a huge, wide-open heart, and that she wanted more than anything to lovingly intertwine her life with the life of someone else. Anyone else. I sensed she was holding me in that big heart of hers, and it felt good. I knew her indiscriminate love had crashed her into disillusionment time and again, but at that point, she was loving me, and that was all that mattered.

Unattractive, ungainly Suzette was an undying romantic, the goddess Aphrodite in an unfortunate body. She liked to pretend that Eldon was the love of her life, and she breathed as much magic into that relationship as she possibly could.

"Oh my God, Lanie!" she said one day. "When he made love to me last night, he made my eyeballs roll back in my head!"

But on her bad days, when her blood sugar had sky-rocketed or when the pain in her legs had risen to excruciating proportions, she'd tell me her husband was nothing but a schmuck. Eldon sat in front of the TV after dinner, barely speaking to her all evening. Eldon didn't cuddle with her after lovemaking. He'd roll over and start snoring seconds after they were done. Eldon acted like a dork in social settings, and he didn't know how to hold conversations. Eldon embarrassed her.

"He never pays attention to me," she'd whine. "I just want somebody to pay attention to me."

I wanted to tell her she had my attention, but I knew that wasn't enough. It had to come from a man.

Suzette would tell me about her secret infatuations with other men and the X-rated dreams she had about them. "What did you think about Jim Halverson at the dance class?" she asked, her tongue flicking lasciviously around her lips.

I'd never thought of Mr. Halverson, who read scripture and led prayers at St. Augustine's, as a sexy man. "He's nice-looking, I guess."

"Did you notice his cute little butt? I could hardly take my eyes off it. Every time he walked past me, I just wanted to reach out and grab it." She punished her naughty impulse by slapping one hand with the other.

"Gee, thanks," I said. "Now when I see Mr. Halverson at church, I won't be able to keep a straight face. I'll be thinking about his butt under that acolyte robe."

There were countless other players in her fantasy life. On and on she'd go, regaling me with the lurid details of her imagination.

Suddenly, she'd stop, as if jolted back to harsh reality. "But who would want this?" she'd say, pointing to her homely face.

I never knew what to say to Suzette when she talked like that. I wanted to promise her that someday, some guy would fall madly in love with her, but she and I both knew that wasn't going to happen. I also wanted to point out that, as far as I could tell, her life with the lackluster Eldon was more stable than it had ever been, and that if not for Eldon's hard-earned money, she wouldn't have the luxury of her messy basement studio. But saying that would have been insensitive to her angst.

CHAPTER 10

One Saturday afternoon in late October, I sat in Suzette's studio helping her paint a batch of baby duck figurines for an upcoming craft fair. "So what happened to you and your ex-husband?" she asked out of the blue. "What did you say his name was?"

I put the last stroke of bright yellow basecoat on my duck, and then set it aside to dry so Suzette could add the detail of long-lashed cartoon eyes. "Kevin," I replied. "His name is Kevin."

"Kevin," she repeated. "Good name for a louse."

"I'm not saying he was a louse," I objected. "It just didn't work out between us."

"How's come?"

I didn't want to air my marital problems. I knew Suzette would jump on them and make more out of them than what was there. So I tried to choose my words carefully. "We got along okay. But Kevin said there wasn't any chemistry in our relationship."

Suzette snorted. "That was a stupid thing to say. Sounds like an excuse to me. Was he cheating on you?"

Startled, I looked up at her, unable to believe how quickly she'd gotten to the heart of the matter. "Yes," I said, "he was."

"Then he is a louse. So what did you do, rip up his clothes and throw him out of the house?"

"No, he left on his own."

"Well, I hope you gave him a swift kick in the ass on his way out the door." She sighed. "But I bet you didn't. You're too easy-going, Lanie. We need to get some fire in your belly."

I'd had enough of her probing into my personal life, and I retreated into silence, focusing all my attention on the baby ducks.

But Suzette wasn't finished. "Was Kevin good in bed?" she asked, smirking.

"I don't even know how to answer that," I snapped.

"He was the only man you ever slept with, wasn't he, Lanie?"

My face burned with embarrassment, and I kept my head down, saying nothing.

"Wasn't he?" Suzette persisted.

I nodded without looking up at her.

"Well, girl, we're gonna have to get you back out there and get you some more experience."

I refused to respond to her comment. Suzette seemed to know she'd pushed me too far, and was quiet for a minute.

Then she said, "Lanie, I don't want you to take this wrong. You're cute, but I think we could make you cuter. I've been looking at you all afternoon, and you know what I've noticed? It seems like your hair, your eyes, and your skin all sort of blend together. Nothing stands out. It makes you look mousy."

Feeling terribly hurt and humiliated, I wanted to scream at her to leave me alone. I wanted to hurl a baby duck at her and hit her right between her ugly old eyes. But I sat quietly stroking yellow paint on the back of a duckling, as if I hadn't heard her.

"We could change the color of your hair," she continued. "Maybe go with a darker brown. It would make your blue eyes really pop."

"I'm fine with the way it is," I mumbled.

Suzette shrugged. "Just trying to help, Lanie."

On my way home, I gave vent to my frustration, crying and pounding my steering wheel. I didn't know whether I was angry with Suzette, or whether I was fed up with being a mousy-haired woman who didn't know how to kick a man out of her life with flair.

In any case, my car refused to turn into my own driveway, and I drove right past my house and on down into Nashville, where I stopped at the CVS pharmacy. There, I stood in front of the display of hair dye, and through a blur of tears, I tried to make sense of the different brands and colors.

Then my eyes focused on a box featuring a beautiful, blue-eyed, fair-skinned woman with a gorgeous mane of reddish-brown hair. The shade was listed as *Dark Auburn Brown*.

On impulse, I picked up the box and headed toward the checkout lane.

As soon as I got home, I went straight to my bathroom and applied the new color to my hair. I figured if it didn't work out, I'd pull a stocking cap over my ruined hair and run to the pharmacy for a different shade.

But the new color turned out splendidly. As I gazed at myself in the bathroom mirror, turning this way and that to admire my reflection from different angles, I knew Suzette had been right.

Two days later, I made a long overdue trip to my hair salon and had my long, limp locks trimmed and styled in a perky, shoulder-length hairdo.

The next time Suzette greeted me at her front door, she pretended to swoon from shock. Then she took my face in her hands and kissed me on the forehead.

"Absolutely exquisite," she said. "Lanie, you've transformed yourself into a beautiful woman."

While we worked in her basement that afternoon, Suzette was quiet, and the contemplative look on her face made me think she was cooking up some kind of plan. Finally, she spoke. "What are you doing for Thanksgiving, Lanie?"

"Going to my grandmother's," I replied. "I always do."

"Oh." Suzette sounded disappointed. "I was hoping you could have Thanksgiving dinner with us."

The usual nerve-wracking holiday routine at Nana's house flashed through my mind: Nana's fussing over the food and the table setting, all the while pummeling my mother and me with a steady barrage of subtle putdowns. Suddenly, the idea of an alternative, any alternative, sounded appealing. "I wish I could," I said.

"Why don't you, then?"

"Nana will have a fit if I'm not there."

Suzette looked at me quizzically, squinting one eye. "How old are you, Lanie?"

"I'll be thirty-one next week."

"Don't you think that's old enough to decide what you want to do?"

CHAPTER 11

The longer I kept company with the outrageous Suzette, the more I sensed a showdown with my grandmother was coming. I could feel something rumbling and heaving in the core of my being.

I showed up at Nana's for my birthday dinner wearing a bright red sweater. "I like your hair," my mother said, fingering her own drab locks.

Those days, my grandmother limited my birthday guests to family members, her two brothers, Harvey and Melvin, and their wives, Clarinda and Dora Mae. Aunt Clarinda, who was heading down the fast-track toward full-blown dementia, took my hand in both of hers. "Do I know you?" she asked, peering intently into my face, completely missing the point that I was the birthday girl.

"Clarinda, that's my granddaughter Elaine," Nana chimed in. "She doesn't look like herself since she changed her hair. Evidently, her natural color isn't good enough anymore."

Nana's blatant hypocrisy stunned me. I glanced around to see if anyone else had picked up on what she'd said, and I saw something flicker in my mother's eyes. I'd seen pictures of Nana in her youth, and I knew she'd been a brunette. No doubt, she'd now be gray if she would allow her natural color to emerge. But ever since I could remember, her twice-monthly trips to the salon had kept her hair platinum blonde.

"That's a lot of candles," Uncle Melvin observed as Nana presided over the lavishly decorated chocolate cake.

"Can you believe it, Melvin?" she chuckled. "My granddaughter is thirty-one."

"Arlene, you don't look old enough to have a thirty-one-year-old grandchild," Aunt Dora Mae warbled.

Nana smiled coyly, patting her plump cheek. "I guess I'm fortunate to be blessed with good skin."

I suddenly felt sorry for the wrinkly-faced, saggy-jowled relatives sitting around the table beaming at her. Once again, Nana had managed to make herself the center of attention, the object of everyone's admiration.

After we ate, Harvey and Melvin dozed in their chairs. Clarinda and Dora Mae fluttered around the kitchen with Nana, trying to help her clean up. As I listened to Nana issuing patronizing orders to the poor old dears, I knew I couldn't take anymore. I decided I'd put in enough time at my birthday party.

I knew it would be rude not to poke my head into the kitchen to thank Nana and say goodbye to my great-aunts. But the anger brewing inside me overpowered my sense of propriety. "I need to go now," I said to my mother.

"I'll see you at Thanksgiving, honey," she said wistfully, giving me a hug. "I don't see you much anymore."

"I won't be here, Mom," I said. "I have other plans."

On that cue, Nana marched into the living room. "Sit down, Elaine," she commanded. "It's not time to go yet."

I stood with my hand on the doorknob for a full thirty seconds, meeting her stern gaze before I relented and seated myself on the edge of the sofa. My mother shot me a worried look before she left the room.

Nana stood in front of me, hands on her hips, her big belly thrust out aggressively. I'd been frightened by that intimidating posture a thousand times before, but this time, it enraged me.

"Elaine, I don't know what's gotten into you recently," she said, shaking her head in disgust.

"What are you talking about?" I asked, even though I

knew full well what she was getting at.

"You seem to be going through some kind of rebellion."

I tried unsuccessfully to keep the sarcasm out of my voice. "Nana, if you want to talk with me, why don't you sit down, too?"

She looked startled by my impertinent, although reasonable, request. "Okay," she said, seating herself on the other end of the sofa.

"I don't know what you're worried about," I said. "I'm not doing anything wrong. I'm not in trouble. I'm not breaking the law. I'm not doing anything that isn't my God-given right to do."

Nana slowly and deliberately shifted her position on the sofa, turning to face me fully. "Don't be smart with me, Elaine. You know what I'm talking about. You haven't been here for two months. And I just heard you tell your mother you're not coming for Thanksgiving."

"I've made other plans."

She shot me a look of sanctimonious outrage. "Other plans for the Thanksgiving holiday? How could you think of turning your back on your family like that?"

"I'm not turning my back on my family. I'm just doing something I want to do."

"I know young people get ideas in their heads about doing their own thing." She spat out the words derisively. "They don't understand the value of family relationships until they get themselves into trouble, and then they expect their family to bail them out. Your mother went through her own little rebellion when she was a teenager. Look at what it got her."

Fury welled in my abdomen, then shot up through my throat and exploded out of my mouth. "It got her me!" I shouted. "That's what you're saying, Nana. It got her me!"

For a second, I glimpsed fear in my grandmother's eyes, but her face quickly took on an expression I knew all too well: condescending, self-righteous disapproval. "You know that's not what I'm saying, Elaine. You know I don't resent the fact that you were born. But your mother's decisions resulted in her getting pregnant by someone she barely knew, and then at eighteen, she was already a widow. That's not something I'd wish on anyone."

"Well, Nana," I huffed. "I'm not eighteen and I'm not pregnant. I'm a full-grown adult, living on my own."

"Adults still need families." Nana's eyes narrowed, fixing me with a penetrating stare. "Just where do you think you'd be, Elaine, if I hadn't done all that I've done for you?"

Her point temporarily deflated me, and I looked down at my hands, studying the tiny red roses Suzette had painted on the tips of my fingernails. But a moment later, I looked up and calmly met her gaze. "I appreciate everything you've done for me, Nana. But if you wouldn't have done it, I would've made my way, somehow."

She snorted. "What makes you think that?"

"Because I'm that kind of person."

I had no idea where those words came from, but saying them felt wonderful. Never in my life had I dared to claim that kind of strength.

"Because I'm that kind of person," I repeated.

Nana knew I'd just delivered the punch-line to our conversation. But she always had to get in the last word, no matter how mean and petty it made her sound.

"Your nails look ridiculous," she hissed. "And that red sweater makes you look washed out." She got up and stalked off to the kitchen.

"I think I look great in red," I called after her.

CHAPTER 12

I had assumed I'd be the only guest invited to Eldon and Suzette's Thanksgiving dinner, but when I arrived at their home, I discovered they were also hosting three young men.

One of them, a slender gentleman in his early thirties, opened the door for me. He was neatly dressed in khaki trousers and a dark sweater.

"Come in," he said in an indifferent tone of voice.

"I'm Elaine," I said. "Suzette's expecting me."

"She said you were coming. She's in the kitchen." Without introducing himself, he retreated to Suzette's recliner and picked up the *Field & Stream* magazine he'd apparently been reading.

The other two young men, grubby fellows in ragged blue jeans, were sprawled on the floor watching television. One was heavy-set, his ill-fitting tee shirt stretched tightly over his ample belly. He wore a baseball cap and sported what looked like an attempt at a goatee. His skinny companion wore a threadbare flannel shirt with the elbows ripped out. A red bandana was tied over his straggly, shoulder-length hair.

Caught off guard by the unexpected circumstances I'd walked into, I stood immobilized, not knowing what to do with myself. But a moment later, Suzette came out of the kitchen.

"Would you guys turn that TV down?" she barked at the two men lounging on the floor. "I'm trying to talk here."

"Okay, Aunt Suzie," the baseball cap wearer yelled as he fumbled for the volume button on the remote control.

Then Suzette turned and smiled at me. "Hi, Lanie. I'm so glad you could make it."

She pointed to the young man holding the remote control.

"This is Butch, and that's his brother Larry. Butch and Larry, this is my friend Lanie."

Both young men looked me up and down, grinning lasciviously. "Pleased to meet you, ma'am," Butch said with contrived stupidity. Larry emitted a laugh that sounded like a snorting pig.

"Knock it off, guys!" Suzette scolded.

Then she turned to the man in the recliner, and her voice softened. "Lanie, this is Eldon's son Kenneth. Kenneth, this is Lanie."

Kenneth barely glanced up from his magazine. I realized he looked a great deal like his father: same thin frame, same dark hair with the same pattern of balding. But Kenneth's face was missing his father's goofy grin, and I could tell he didn't possess Eldon's creepy charm.

"Kenneth works in tech support at Columbus Hospital," Suzette announced proudly. Kenneth raised one eyebrow, seemingly unaffected by her admiration.

"Well, I'll let you guys get acquainted," she said. "I need to get back in the kitchen and help Eldon. He's the chief cook around here."

I had no inclination to stay with the occupants of the living room. The taciturn Kenneth clearly had nothing to say to me, while the grinning Butch and Larry looked like they were ready to pounce on me. So I followed Suzette into the kitchen.

Eldon was up to his elbows in dishwater. I thought I might escape his lingering hug, but when he saw me, he reached for a towel and dried his hands. "Welcome, Lanie," he said, wrapping his arms around me. "I'm so happy you can have dinner with us. I've got a twenty-pound bird in the oven."

Suzette put me to work setting the dining room table. I was glad to have something to do. As I headed back into the kitchen to get a load of plates, I heard a crash coming from the living room, followed by cursing. Suzette dropped her potato masher and rushed out to sée what was happening.

"Would you guys knock it off?" she yelled. "Butch and Larry, you're not kids anymore. You need to start behaving like adults!"

"Sorry, Aunt Suzy," Butch said.

"When are we gonna eat, Aunt Suzy?" Larry whined. "I'm starving."

"Well, you're gonna have to wait," Suzette snapped.

"Those damn boys!" she muttered as she came back into the kitchen.

"What did they do now?" Eldon asked, exasperation in his voice.

"They were horsing around and knocked the lamp off the end table. Nothing got broken."

"Are they your nephews?" I asked.

"No," she said. "Thank God. I let them call me Aunt Suzy because they need a positive female figure in their lives."

"I don't know why you invited them here today," Eldon complained.

"Well, they didn't have anywhere else to go." Suzette turned to me to give a fuller explanation. "Their mother ran off and left them when they were little boys. Their dad raised them, but he's loser, and he's in prison now. They've never had anyone to show them how to live like civilized human beings. I do my best, but I swear, sometimes I think they're hopeless cases."

"They are hopeless cases," Eldon said. "I've been telling you that all along."

Suzette sighed. "Well, I have to try. Butch seems to have half a brain in his head, but Larry's dumber than a box of rocks."

I made several more trips between the kitchen and the dining room, carrying dishes, silverware and napkins. Each time I walked out to the dining room, Butch and Larry looked at each other and rolled around on the floor, laughing. Once when I had my back turned to them, I heard scuffling behind me, and then I felt a hard pinch on my bottom.

I jumped and yelped. Butch muttered something obscene, and Larry burst into snorting laughter.

Quick as a wink, Suzette was out of the kitchen again. I didn't turn around to see what was happening, but I could hear the sound of a hand smacking flesh. Butch yelled, "Ouch!"

"YOU KEEP YOUR FILTHY HANDS OFF HER!" Suzette bellowed. "She's not for you, you little creep!"

I was glad for Suzette's swift intervention, although the whole scenario was more amusing than threatening. Then I began to wonder who she thought I was for. Suddenly, it dawned on me: Kenneth. This invitation to Thanksgiving dinner was a setup for me to meet Suzette's stepson. If the idea hadn't been so ludicrous, I would have been angry.

When dinner was ready, Suzette told us all where to sit around the table, and of course, she placed me next to Kenneth. In an attempt to make polite conversation, I asked him, "So you work in tech support?"

He nodded. I waited for him to reciprocate with a socially appropriate question, and when he didn't, I said, "I'm a massage therapist."

"A massage therapist," he said. "Hmm." And that was the extent of our conversation for the day.

The Thanksgiving meal wasn't nearly as tasty as what I would have been served at Nana's house. The turkey was dry, the cranberry salad was watery, the green beans were under-seasoned, and Eldon had completely forgotten to make gravy for the mashed potatoes. But I told myself I wouldn't want to be anywhere else that Thanksgiving Day. I'd begun to enjoy the odd assortment of characters engaged in their weird little drama.

Queen Suzette, wearing a ratty harvest-gold sweater embellished with orange pumpkins, presided over the mediocre spread with all the dignity she could muster. She'd arranged a centerpiece for the table, silk autumn leaves surrounding a pair of pilgrim figurines that I'd sculpted and she'd molded. She insisted that her two oafish protégés remove their headwear before sitting down at the table.

"This ain't a hat, it's a do-rag," Larry complained.

Suzette looked him dead in the eye. "Here's the way it is, Larry. If you want to sit down and eat with us, you'll take it off."

I bit my lip to keep from laughing every time she barked at the poor fellow for chewing with his mouth open. "Good God, Larry," she'd say. "I don't need to see the entire contents of your mouth."

When Butch emitted a loud belch, she demanded that he apologize. "Sorry, Aunt Suzy," he said.

But Suzette wasn't satisfied. "What are you supposed to say when you belch?"

"I already said I was sorry."

"Damn it, Butch, you're supposed to say *excuse me* when you belch. At this table, we say *excuse me.*"

"Well, excuse me!" he snapped.

"That's better," she huffed.

After dinner, Butch and Larry said they had somewhere they needed to go. Suzette eyed them suspiciously. "You guys better not be up to something that's gonna land you in trouble."

They both adamantly denied any nefarious intentions, and off they roared in their muffler-free junk-heap of a car.

After Butch and Larry left, I helped Suzette clear the table while Eldon got out an oversized wooden *Aggravation* board. "He made that out there in his garage," Suzette said. "Pretty good, huh?"

Then she, Eldon, Kenneth, and I sat down to play the game. That's when I discovered how truly charmless Suzette's stepson was.

Eldon took every opportunity to congratulate me on good moves, reaching over to pat my arm or rub my shoulder. "Way to go, Lanie," he'd say. But Kenneth seemed barely aware of my presence across the table from him. As he mechanically moved his marbles around the game board, he looked bored, as aloof as he'd been throughout the rest of the day's activities.

After one game, I told Suzette I had to leave. "Come down to my studio," she said. "I need to give you some more clay."

As soon as we were out of the men's earshot, Suzette grinned broadly. "So what did you think of Kenneth, Lanie? He's a nice guy, isn't he? And he makes damn good money."

"Suzette," I said. "Kenneth's not interested in me. He barely spoke to me all afternoon."

"Oh, he's just a little shy around women. You should've given him a little more encouragement."

"I don't think Kenneth is my type."

She shot me a stern look. "Lanie, you need to come out and say what you mean. If you're not interested in Kenneth, just tell me."

"Sorry, Suzette. I'm not interested in Kenneth."

"Well, thank you for being honest. We'll just have to find you someone else."

She began rummaging around the studio for the clay she'd promised me, but seemed to lose her focus. She picked up a few paintbrushes and stuffed them into a can, and then moved some wooden pieces from one side of the table to the other. "There's something I want to do with you, Lanie. But not today. I'm too tired."

Suddenly, she started to swoon, and she grasped the table for support. Sinking into a chair, she whispered, "Lanie, before you go, will you tell Eldon to come down here? I'm going to need help getting up the stairs."

CHAPTER 13

I was worried about Suzette, and the next day, I called to see if she was okay.

"I'm fine," she said. "I just overdid it yesterday. Too much bullshit going on around me."

"You told me you wanted to do something with me," I reminded her. "What is it?"

"Well, Lanie, you're just going to have to wait and see," she said in the same scolding tone she used with Butch and Larry.

A week later, I drove to Suzette's house to deliver the sculpted nativity figures I'd been working on the past month. This had been my most ambitious project to date, and I was sure she'd be thrilled with what I'd done.

We sat together in her studio as she methodically inspected each piece. "Very nice," she finally said. "I don't see any problems. I think you've got the hang of this now."

Her subdued response deflated me. "When are you going to mold them?" I asked.

She sighed deeply as she put down the figure of the shepherd she was holding. "I was hoping I'd get them molded and finished up for Christmas sales this year, but I don't think I'm going to make it. This will have to be next year's project."

I must have looked as dejected as I felt, because she said, "I'm not upset with you, Lanie. I'm upset with myself. I'm not able to work as fast as I used to."

She took a deep breath and then smiled, as if trying to pump up her own spirits. "We'll just have to do something else instead."

So we turned our attention to painting large wooden angels Eldon had cut out with his scroll saw. "I'll put some of these in the shop in Nashville," she told me. "And a friend of mine attends that little country church on Gatesville Road, east of Bean Blossom. They always have an awesome holiday bazaar, and I told my friend I'd donate something. Never hurts to do a good deed, you know."

As usual, I painted the basecoats, and then passed the pieces on to Suzette to do the detail work. All the while, I kept wondering about the mysterious activity she had planned for the two of us. Finally, I ventured to satisfy my curiosity. "What was it you wanted to do . . . ?

"Just be patient," she interrupted in an irritable tone. "We'll get to it. I really need to get these done. If we don't get them painted today, then it'll probably never happen."

So I held my tongue and waited. Two hours later, Suzette sighed with relief as she carefully laid the last painted angel on the table to dry. "There. I think they look wonderful. We do good work together, don't we, Lanie?"

I was determined not to aggravate her by once again bringing up the subject of the mystery activity, so I picked up my coat from the back of my chair and said, "Well, I'll see you next week."

"Don't go yet, Lanie." Suzette pointed to the doorway of a small room adjacent to her studio. "Let's go in there."

I'd been aware of that room, but had never entered it, and had never given it much thought. As far as I could tell, it was filled with the same kind of junk that cluttered her studio, and I'd assumed Suzette used it as overflow storage.

As I followed her into the dank room, which was illuminated only by the daylight coming through one small window, I saw that my assumption had been partially correct.

The periphery of the small space was crammed full of old furniture, cardboard boxes, and piles of craft supplies. My eyes fell on the kiln in the far corner of the room. *Of course,* I thought. *This is where Suzette fires her ceramic pieces.*

In the center of the room stood a small table draped with a red velvet cloth. A taper candle wedged into an old wine bottle served as the table's only ornament.

"This is my meditation room." Suzette gestured with a grand wave of her hand, as if introducing me to a magnificent hall in a stately palace. "I come down here to meditate when I get stressed out. I should do it more often."

One battered folding chair was pulled up to the table. Suzette moved around a few boxes, and then pulled out an old armchair with torn upholstery. "Have a seat, Lanie," she said.

Reaching for a book of matches lying on a stack of scrap plywood, she lit the candle, and then seated herself on the folding chair opposite me.

"Have you ever meditated, Lanie?" she asked.

"No," I admitted.

"Well, I'm going to teach you how. I learned this when I lived in California. Rest your hands on your thighs, palms down. Make sure you're sitting up straight. You need to have a straight spine for meditation."

I obligingly placed my hands in the proper position and sat as straight as the broken-down chair would allow.

"Now let's breathe together," she said. "Take a deep breath, very slowly. Then let it out slowly. Just keep that up, and you'll start to relax. You can close your eyes if you want to, or you can focus on the candle flame. Either way is okay. Try to keep your mind on something spiritual, like love or peace."

I didn't feel comfortable closing my eyes, so I stared at the candle flame, pacing my breathing with Suzette's slow, labored breathing. The flickering candlelight bathed her face in a soft glow, making her homely features seem perfect and beautiful.

Within minutes, I felt deeply relaxed, and I sensed something descending over the two of us, a mist of gentle, blissful peace. I felt as if I never wanted to leave that moment, Suzette's presence, or that messy little candlelit room.

After awhile, Suzette opened her eyes and smiled at me. "How'd you like that, Lanie?" she asked.

I exhaled deeply. "It was really nice."

She glanced at her watch. "We meditated for fifteen minutes. That's really good for a beginner. I think you're a natural, Lanie. Some people don't take to this kind of thing at all."

"Really?" I said. "You think I'm a natural at this?"

"Absolutely," Suzette responded. "Whether you know it or not, Lanie, you're a deeply spiritual person."

"Really?" I repeated. Suzette nodded, smiling.

I glanced around the cluttered room, trying to shake off the meditation daze and come back to my normal senses. "Well, I guess I'd better get going."

"Not yet," Suzette said. "There's something else I want to do."

With considerable effort, she eased her heavy body out of her chair and limped over to the window, where she grabbed a black velvet pouch off the sill. Then she sat down at the table again. Moving the candle to one side, she slid a deck of cards out of the bag.

"Tarot cards," she said. "A woman in California taught me how to use them. I want to do a reading on you, Lanie. Do you have a question you want us to focus on?"

Caught off guard, I said, "I can't think of anything."

Suzette hesitated, eyes downcast as if deep in thought. "Let's ask about your love life," she finally said. "Let's see if you're going to meet someone."

I watched, transfixed, as with great dignity and deliberation, Suzette laid out the mysterious cards with the strange figures on them. At times, she murmured something under her breath.

Finally, she laid down the last card, and then looked up at me, beaming. "I can't say I know everything about reading tarot cards. I lost the instruction book the woman in California gave me. But, Lanie, I'm sure about this. These cards say that love is coming to you. A man is going to enter your life, someone who will be very important to you."

"How can you be sure?" I asked.

"I have a gut feeling about it, too. Honey, you're on the verge of something wonderful."

I must have looked bewildered, because she expounded on her statement. "By gut feeling, I mean intuition. I've learned to trust my intuition. I let it guide me. It's hardly ever wrong."

I wasn't at all convinced that Suzette's strange cards and her gut feeling could accurately predict anything about my love life, but I didn't want to spoil the magic of the moment. "Wow!" I exclaimed. "I'm so excited!" Then I added, "So when is this supposed to happen?"

She gazed at me over the top of her bifocals. "When you least expect it, Lanie. When you least expect it. We'll just have to wait and see."

As I stood up to leave, I asked, "Can we do this again? Meditate, I mean."

"Of course we'll meditate again!" Suzette laid her graceful, pink-nailed hand on my arm. "Lanie, we're partners. Not just artistic partners. Spiritual partners, too."

She hesitated, and I saw a flicker of pain in her eyes. "At least for now."

Then she smiled. "But I think for always."

CHAPTER 14

As I drove to the Nashville IGA on a Monday evening in January, I knew I should have taken the weatherman more seriously. Heavy, wet snowflakes pelted my windshield, and when I stopped at the traffic light in the center of town, my car slid into the intersection. *Just hurry and get your shopping done,* I told myself. *You've got to get home before conditions get worse.*

The four or five vehicles in the IGA parking lot told me the store was nearly empty. Through the rapidly accumulating snow cover, I sloshed my way to the entry door and grabbed a shopping cart.

Rushing through the produce section, I grabbed a bag of oranges and a head of lettuce. I made a quick stop at the deli, ordering a container of tuna salad. As I headed down Aisle 2 to pick up some soup and crackers, I saw an extraordinarily tall man coming toward me, pushing a half-filled shopping cart. I estimated his height to be to be 6'6" or 6'7". He was a remarkably handsome gentleman with a thick mane of silver hair. I wondered why I'd never seen him around Nashville. His striking appearance would have been hard to miss.

The man gave me a nod as we passed each other. Less than a minute later, he passed me again while I was reaching for a box of cereal in Aisle 4. This time, he flashed me a boyish smile. I realized he wasn't as old as his gray hair suggested, perhaps only a few years older than me.

When we approached each other in the paper goods aisle, he laughed and said, "I guess we're destined to keep on meeting." Then he peered at me intently. "You went to Brown County High School, didn't you?"

I found his question odd, as nearly every adult in town had once attended Brown County High. But I said, "Yes, I did."

"What year did you graduate?"

"1996."

"Oh," he said, "you're Elaine Greene. You were two years behind me."

I stared at him, bewildered.

"Don't you recognize me?" he asked. "I'm J. J."

Suddenly, his handsome face connected with an image in my memory bank. "Oh, yes!" I exclaimed. "You're Jesse Jordan!"

My mind raced back sixteen years to my sophomore year of high school. Jesse Jordan had been a senior and the center on the varsity basketball team. That had been the year of Jesse Jordan, the year BCHS won the regionals in the state tourney. I recalled sitting in the bleachers among hoards of Jesse fans, clapping my hands and chanting the initials of the dark-haired Adonis who towered over all the other players on the court, both in height and in ability.

I'd never spoken to Jesse Jordan when I was in high school. I wouldn't have dreamed of making a social overture to someone whose status was so far above mine. But there I was, chatting with him in the grocery store, standing face to face with this demigod, closer than I ever stood to him during my high school years.

"I'm sorry," I said. "I didn't recognize you at first."

He grinned, running his big hand through his thick hair. "This gray throws people off."

"Well, I've probably changed, too."

"I'd say you've gotten prettier." He flashed me another charming smile.

"How did you know my name?" I asked. "I didn't even think you knew my name in high school."

"I knew everyone," he said.

I stood there staring up at this giant of a man, while he smiled down on me. "I'd better get going," I finally said. "I need to get home before the snow gets too deep."

Instead of passing on by, Jesse made a U-turn with his shopping cart. "We might as well travel in the same direction."

Unnerved by the sound of his cart clattering behind me, I decided against looking for the rest of the groceries on my list and headed straight toward the checkout lane. Jesse followed me.

As the cashier scanned my groceries, I looked out the window and saw that the snowstorm had escalated to blizzard conditions. "I hope I don't get stuck in my driveway," I fretted.

"I'll follow you home and make sure you get in okay," a voice behind me said. "My truck's got four-wheel drive."

Ordinarily, I never would have consented to being followed home by a man I didn't know well. But at that moment, it looked as if the weather posed a far greater risk to me than did Jesse Jordan. "Okay," I said.

As I drove home, I repeatedly checked my rearview mirror, each time seeing Jesse's reassuring headlights shining through the blinding snow. As it turned out, I got stuck before I made it halfway down my long driveway. Jesse pulled in behind me and jumped out of his truck.

"Got a shovel?" he asked.

Together, we trudged through the deep drifts, slowly making our way to my garage to find what we needed. Jesse laughed lightheartedly, as if enjoying the adventure. "This is pretty crazy, huh?"

Then, from the shelter of my garage, I watched him quickly and effortlessly toss aside huge shovelfuls of snow.

Within minutes, he'd cleared a path for me. He stood beside my driveway while I pulled my car into the garage. Then I came back out to thank him.

"I don't know what I would've done if I hadn't met you in the store," I said as I looked up at him in the swirling snow.

He gazed down on me, the garage light illuminating the earnest expression on his handsome face. "Maybe it was destiny."

I suddenly felt nervous. "Well, thanks again. Be careful on your drive home."

Jesse didn't budge. "Can I call you sometime?" he asked.

At that moment, something felt off-kilter to me. Men like Jesse Jordan dated fashion models and pageant queens, not ordinary girls like me. Sixteen years ago, he wouldn't have given me a second glance. Why was he so interested in me now?

But I couldn't refuse him after the heroic deed he'd just performed on my behalf. "Sure," I said. "Let me go into the house to get something to write my number on.

"Just tell it to me," he said. "I have perfect memory."

Thirty minutes later, my phone rang, and I picked it up to hear Jesse Jordan's cheerful voice on the other end of the line. "I just wanted to let you know I made it home okay. I know you were concerned."

"Well, thanks for telling me," I said.

"Have a good night, Elaine. I'll call you tomorrow."

As I hung up the phone, I thought about Suzette's tarot card prediction. Could this tall, handsome man who'd stepped into my life out of nowhere be the one?

CHAPTER 15

One week later, Jesse Jordan and I met at Nashville's Creekside Pizza Shack for our first date. As I sat with him at our rustic wooden table, I barely had a chance to talk to him, as I was forced to share him with a steady stream of his former fans. Each time someone approached our table, his handsome face lit up with pleasure. I could see how much he enjoyed the spotlight.

"Where've you been all these years, J. J.?" one man asked as he heartily pumped Jesse's hand.

"Here, there, and everywhere," Jesse said, laughing.

Another man clapped him on the shoulder and said, "Good to see you, J. J. When did you get back in town?"

"Around the first of December," Jesse responded.

"What brings you back here to Nashville?"

"I decided I wanted to be closer to my family."

"Where are you living now?"

"I'm staying with my sister in Gnawbone, but I'm looking for a place of my own."

When the traffic of admirers finally died down, I found myself sitting across the table from a somber-faced date who seemed to have nothing to say to me.

"So you just moved back here," I said, attempting to start conversation. "It's no wonder I haven't seen you around town. Where were you living before?"

"Fort Wayne."

"What were you doing there?"

"Same thing I'm doing now, driving a UPS truck."

"You got transferred here?"

"Yup, they got me working out of Columbus now."

"So you could be closer to your family?"

Jesse's face darkened, and he glared at me as if I'd accused him of something heinous. "What is this, you giving me the third degree? What's wrong with wanting to be closer to family?"

"Nothing," I said. "Nothing at all."

I was afraid to ask him any more questions for fear of stepping on another landmine. The waitress set our pizza on the table. I picked up a slice and took a bite, and then filled the stony silence by exclaiming how delicious it was.

Thankfully, the tension between us was broken when another fan approached Jesse, clapped him on the back, and engaged him in a few minutes of basketball conversation.

After the man walked away, Jesse turned back to me. "Sorry I got snappy. I know being a UPS driver isn't much of a job. It doesn't impress women."

"I think it's a fine job," I said. "I don't have a problem with it. In this economy, a lot of people would feel lucky to have a job like yours."

His handsome face looked glum again. "I know, but I could've done so much more with my life. I had a full basketball scholarship to IU. But I blew it the first year. I partied, flunked all my classes. Stupidest thing I ever did. I could've gone all the way to the pros. But look at me now."

"You're not the only one who dropped out of college," I said in an effort to cheer him up. "I started out as an art major, and it was a total bust. I didn't even make it through the first year."

Jesse looked at me intently, as if noticing me for the first time. "What do you do now?"

"I'm a massage therapist."

"Did you have to go to school for that?"

"Yes, I did a one-year program."

"So you ended up making something out of yourself."

"So did you," I said, trying to keep the irritation out of my voice. "Being a UPS driver is a darned good job."

"Not good enough for me," he said.

I gave up all hope of having a congenial conversation with this man, and focused my attention back on the pizza. Fortunately, we were interrupted once again, this time by Jesse's former teammate, Rick.

Jesse jumped up to greet him, and the two men hugged and thumped each other on the back. Then, for a full ten minutes, they carried on a boisterous conversation, reminiscing about their glory days on Brown County High's varsity basketball team.

Feeling bored and left out, I decided to use the opportunity to make a trip to the ladies' room. A girl I knew in high school rushed up to me, giddy with excitement. "You're dating Jesse Jordan?" she asked, incredulous.

"I can't really say I'm dating him," I replied. "This is the first time I've been out with him."

"Well, you'd better hang on to him. A lot of us are jealous, you know."

When I came back to the table, Rick gave Jesse a jovial punch on the arm and said, "Well, I'd better let you get back to your date." I realized Jesse hadn't even introduced us.

The encounter with his old friend seemed to have lightened Jesse's mood. Grinning from ear to ear, he leaned across the table and said, "Remember when Rick put that playboy centerfold on the chemistry teacher's periodical chart?"

I laughed and said, "No, I hadn't heard about that."

So he regaled me with the details, old Mr. Watson's beet-red face and the chemistry students' lewd comments. Then he kept me laughing, telling one funny story after another, mostly about the pranks his teammates pulled on each other.

"That Rick was a terror," he said, shaking his head. "Almost got himself kicked off the basketball team."

But then his mood turned dark again as his stories cycled around to his college failure and his lost career opportunities. At the end of the date, I concluded that Jesse Jordan was a self-centered, self-pitying man. I went home exhausted from riding the rollercoaster of his moods and trying to pump up his deflated self-esteem.

If he'd been anyone besides Jesse Jordan, I never would have accepted another date with a man like that. But I had to admit to myself that I enjoyed being seen with this former star, and even if our personal conversations tried my patience, his public persona still charmed me.

Jesse came to my house to pick me up for our second date, and we drove to Bloomington to see a movie at the Indiana University Cinema. We arrived in town twenty minutes early, and Jesse decided to kill time by driving around the campus.

His mood became increasingly edgy as he pointed out familiar sights, spouting sarcastic comments about the good-for-nothing university, the professors who had it in for him, and all the stuck-up students who thought they were better than he was.

I told myself I should have known this would happen if he visited the site of his colossal failure. As I stared morosely out his truck window, trying to tune out his crazy rant, I mentally kicked myself for not having had the sense to decline a second date with this unbearable man.

While we were standing in the theatre's ticket line, Jesse scowled at me and said, "Why did you fix your hair that way? I don't like it pulled back like that. It isn't flattering to your face."

His unthinkable rudeness floored me. For a moment, I stood with my eyes downcast, my face burning with shame, feeling like an eight-year-old withering under Nana's scathing criticism.

But only for a moment. Then I was angry, and I knew I'd had enough of my date's terrible behavior.

Looking up to meet Jesse's sullen gaze, I snapped, "So excuse me for having a bad hair day. If you don't like it, don't look at me."

"You could've worked a little harder on it for my sake," he pouted. "After all, I'm paying for this date."

Shaking with rage, I stepped out of the ticket line. "Then save yourself some money, Jesse Jordan. Buy just one ticket, because I'm leaving."

Without a backward glance, I headed toward the door. I'd taken only a few steps when I felt strong fingers gripping my upper arm like a vice. "Don't leave, Elaine," Jesse hissed in my ear. "Don't embarrass me in front of all these people."

Still holding my arm, his voice softened. "I'm sorry. I was a jerk. I get that way when I'm stressed out. I had a rough day, okay? Please stay, Elaine. Please."

I don't know why I didn't walk out of the theatre and out of Jesse Jordan's life right then and there. Looking back, I think I sensed that choice would have been too risky. Jesse would have made a scene, and later, there might have been more serious consequences.

In any case, I obligingly stepped back into the ticket line. Jesse put his big hands on my shoulders and gently massaged the muscles that were now tight with tension. "Relax, Elaine," he crooned.

Thankfully, our movie was a comedy, and as we laughed together, Jesse became more lighthearted. At one point, he put his arm around the back of my seat and rubbed the spot on my arm where he'd earlier squeezed it. His hand traveled up to caress my neck, and then a big finger gently brushed my cheek as he whispered in my ear, "You're beautiful, Elaine. You're perfect just the way you are. Don't let big jerks like me tell you anything different."

CHAPTER 16

When Jesse called me the following week, he was so cheerful and considerate that I convinced myself his unpleasant behavior at the movie theatre had been an aberration, an exception to his normal congenial personality. He asked me questions about my massage business, making me feel as if he was truly interested in me. I told him about the sculpting I did for Suzette, and how she'd helped me discover that I still had potential as an artist.

"What an inspirational story!" he exclaimed. "You thought you were a failure, but your friend gave you a new start."

Please apply this thought to your own life, I wanted to tell him. *Maybe there's a new beginning for you, too.*

Our third date was on a balmy day in mid-February. We hadn't planned an activity for the evening, and Jesse drove me around in his truck while we discussed what we wanted to do.

"Where does your friend Suzette live?" he suddenly asked.

"Helmsburg."

"Helmsburg!" he chortled. "I haven't been to Helmsburg in ages. Let's drive over there."

"But she's not expecting us," I objected. "I always call before I go."

"Aw, let's just drop by for a few minutes. Surprise her."

Suzette was definitely surprised when she greeted us at the door. She was wearing pajamas and a shabby robe, and her wispy hair looked a fright. She was clearly exhausted, but responded graciously when I introduced her to Jesse. Then she wearily led us down her steep basement stairs to show him where she and I worked together.

Jesse seemed genuinely interested in the various art projects Suzette had lying around, and when she pointed out pieces she and I had done together, he expressed amazement. "You two are awesome!" he gushed.

Then Eldon took us out to his garage to show Jesse where he completed his end of the woodworking projects. As we climbed back into the truck to leave, Jesse said, "Your friends are nice people."

On our way back to my home, the driver in front of us stopped abruptly as we were turning to cross the railroad tracks on State Road 45. Jesse slammed on his brakes and narrowly missed rear-ending him. As I pitched forward in my seat, I screamed involuntarily.

Jesse shot me a malevolent look. "What? You don't have any confidence in my driving?"

"It wasn't your fault," I said. "Sorry. I didn't mean to scream like that."

But the incident sent him into a nasty mood. The rest of the way home, he swore and muttered ugly things under his breath. I turned away from him and stared out the window, knowing that anything I said would only fuel his temper.

"I wasted a whole evening hanging out with those damn hillbillies," he snarled when he pulled into my driveway.

At that point, I knew Jesse Jordan had blown his last chance with me. "I don't date men who insult my friends," I shouted at him. "Don't call me again, Jesse." And with that, I climbed out of his truck.

I heard him say, "I'm sorry . . . ," but I slammed the door shut and rushed into my house.

I spent the next ten minutes pacing around my living room, trying to calm myself. Suddenly, I spotted a flashing red light on my answering machine. When I checked the message, I heard Suzette's voice. "I just wanted to make sure you're all right, honey. Call me when you get this message."

I immediately dialed her number. "Maybe I'm being silly, Lanie," she said, "but I got a weird vibe off that guy."

"I know," I said. "I got the same vibe. I'm not going to see him again."

When I didn't hear from Jesse for three days, I began to relax, thinking I'd succeeded in getting rid of him. But then he called me at ten o'clock on Tuesday evening.

"Jesse," I said when I answered the phone, "I told you not to call me."

"I just wanted to talk through our misunderstanding," he said. "Discuss things like mature adults."

"There's nothing to discuss, Jesse. I'm not interested in a relationship with you."

"You can't cut me off like this, Elaine," he whimpered. "You can't dump a guy for screwing up just one time. None of us are perfect, you know." Then his voice took on an ugly edge. "You're not perfect yourself, Elaine, even though you might think you are."

For five minutes, I listened to him plead and cry. "I'm a broken man, Elaine. I'm going through a rough time in my life, and I need a woman like you to help me get back on my feet. Give me just one more chance. I'll treat you better than any man has ever treated you. I promise."

"Jesse," I said as kindly as I could, "there are plenty of women around Nashville who would love to date you. Go find one of them. I'm not the woman for you. Now I'm hanging up. Please don't call me anymore. If you do, I'm not going to answer the phone."

After I hung up, he called back six times. I let the phone ring until it went to the answering machine, and each time, he left a pleading message. The last time, he sounded calmer. "I'm going to give you some space, Elaine. Maybe you need time to think this over."

On Friday morning, I heard the phone ring while I was in the middle of a massage session. After my client left, I checked the message. It was Jesse, and his voice sounded harsh and threatening.

"You're right, Elaine, it wouldn't work out between us. I lay awake all night thinking about you giving men massages, putting your hands all over them. It makes me sick. Any woman who decides to be a massage therapist is nothing but a dirty whore."

I recoiled in horror. I knew then that Jesse Jordan wasn't just egotistical and self-pitying, he was seriously disturbed. *Oh my God!* I thought. *What have I gotten myself into?*

Around 1:00 o'clock on Saturday morning, I awoke to the sound of my phone ringing. My first thought was that something had happened to my mother or Nana. Feeling dazed and disoriented, I fumbled for the extension on my nightstand.

It was Jesse. "Elaine, I've been thinking things through. I believe we can come to some kind of compromise. Maybe you can agree to take only female massage clients."

"I'm not going to do that," I said. "I have to earn a living. I can't afford to cut my practice in half."

"I could move in with you and help you pay the bills.

Your place looks a little rundown. You could use a man around the house to fix it up."

"You're crazy, Jesse," I said before I hung up the phone.

For the next week, Jesse called me eight to ten times a day, his messages alternating between pleading and threatening. At times when I felt desperate for peace and quiet, I resorted to unplugging my phone. I was reluctant to do that, because my home phone was also my business line, and I hated Jesse for putting me in that predicament.

Then other people began calling me, current friends, former friends, even people I didn't know well. "Are you dating Jesse Jordan?" they'd asked. "He called and said the two of you were having problems."

"I'm not dating him," I'd tell them. "I went out with him a few times, but I'm not seeing him anymore."

"I don't appreciate being put in the middle of your problems," one woman told me.

"I'm so sorry," I said. "Please don't talk to him if he calls you again."

One afternoon, I stopped by the National City Bank to deposit a week's worth of checks from my business. When I stepped up to my mother's teller window, she shot me a coy smile and said, "I didn't know you were dating Jesse Jordan."

Exasperated, I thumped the counter with my fist. "Mom, I'm not dating him! He's telling everybody that, but it isn't true. I told him I don't want to see him anymore. He just won't leave me alone."

My mother looked bewildered. "I'm so sorry, honey. I didn't know. He was in here earlier today. He came over to my window and introduced himself. He said, 'I'm Elaine's boyfriend. I've been looking forward to meeting you.' He said the two of you were having a little misunderstanding, but that you were trying to work it out. I thought it was a little strange, the way he came in to tell me all that, but he was really nice about it."

"Don't talk to him again!" I said. "He's making a terrible nuisance of himself. If he comes in again, don't say anything to him. If he makes a scene, tell him to leave."

The next time Jesse called me, I picked up the phone. "Stop calling my friends and family!" I shouted at him.

"I can talk to whoever I want to," he retorted. "I have to talk to somebody, because you won't listen to reason." He paused, and when he spoke again, I could hear the evil satisfaction in his voice. "The next person I'm going to call is your grandmother."

His words struck terror in my heart, and in my mind's eye, I could see the malevolent smirk on his face. If he called Nana, any meager trust she'd had in my ability to manage my own life would completely dissipate.

"You don't even know her," I snapped.

"I know who she is," he said. "You'd be surprised at everything I know about your life, Elaine Greene."

"Don't you dare call her!" I screamed. "Don't you dare!"

This time, Jesse hung up on me.

One morning when a client walked into my home for her appointment, she asked, "Are you expecting a delivery? There's a UPS truck parked at the edge of your driveway. I barely had room to pull my car through."

I glanced out the window and saw a gray-haired man sitting in the driver's seat of large brown truck.

After ushering my client into the treatment room, I excused myself to make a phone call. I dialed the number of the police department. "Jesse Jordan is sitting in my driveway in his UPS truck," I told the officer. "I don't want him here. I don't want him anywhere near me."

At the end of my massage session, the truck was gone. But that evening, Jesse called me every five minutes, letting the phone ring just a few times before hanging up. I finally unplugged my phone again.

The next day, I called the police department and spoke to a detective, describing in detail how Jesse had behaved the past few weeks.

"You can file harassment charges if you want to," the detective said. "But why don't you let me talk with Jesse first? That'll probably be enough to make him back off."

Twenty-four hours later, the detective called me back. "I brought Jesse in and had a talk with him. He's really distraught about the two of you breaking up. He seems to really care about you. I told him he should cool it and leave you alone for awhile." Then his voice sounded less official. "Why don't you give the poor guy another chance?"

That evening, Jesse screamed into my answering machine, "Even the police department thinks you're being an unreasonable bitch!"

Feeling utterly defeated, I called Suzette. "He's driving me crazy!" I sobbed into the phone. "He's talking about me all over town. He's causing problems with my business. He's ruining my entire life!"

"He's called here a few times," Suzette said. "I just tell him I won't listen to his bullshit and hang up on him. But the next time he calls, I'll take care of it. Don't worry, Lanie, I'll make him leave you alone."

"How are you going to do that?" I sniffled.

"Never you mind, honey. I know what I'm doing. This old broad has been around the block a few times. When I lived in California, I handled bigger problems than Jesse Jordan."

Two days later, Jesse's calls suddenly stopped.

"What did you say to him?" I asked Suzette.

"Never you mind," she said. "Jesse's going to leave you alone now, and you need to get on with your life."

A month later, while I was shopping at the CVS pharmacy, a tall, dark-haired woman approached me near the checkout lane. "Are you Elaine Greene?" she asked.

"Yes," I replied.

She laid a gentle hand on my arm. "I'm Jennifer Jordan. I'm so sorry for what my brother put you through. I tried to make him stop, but he wouldn't listen to me."

Then she told me the story of how Jesse had suffered a mental breakdown during his freshman year at Indiana University. "I've had to keep an eye on him ever since then," she said. "He was really struggling when he lived in Fort Wayne. I was afraid he was on the verge of another breakdown, so I brought him back here to live with me."

Her eyes clouded with pain. "I had no idea what a handful he'd be. I honestly didn't know how I was going to make it over the long haul. But four weeks ago, he came home looking a little roughed up, like he'd been in a fight. He told me he was going to apply for a transfer to Indianapolis. Before I knew it, he was gone. I guess he's doing okay now. It's always up and down with Jesse."

"Do you have thugs working for you?" I asked Suzette the

next time I sat working with her in her basement studio.

She shot me a stern look. "Why on earth would you ask me a stupid question like that, Lanie?"

Turning away from me, she let out an evil little cackle, and then muttered something under her breath that sounded like, "Thugs! Good name for those boys."

"What are you talking about?" I asked.

"Nothing," she replied.

"But I heard you say . . . "

She swung around to face me, her jaw clenched, her owlish eyes large and round with mock fierceness. "I said nothing!"

"Your tarot cards lied," I told her after she'd simmered down a few minutes later. "They said I was going to find love. But then I ran right smack into Jesse Jordan, and all hell broke loose in my life."

Suzette shrugged. "I don't know why the cards say what they say. All I do is read them like I see them. Anyway, they didn't say you weren't going to run into a few duds first."

CHAPTER 17

After the uproar created by Jesse Jordan died down, I enjoyed a spell of peace and serenity that arrived concurrently with spring. During the months of April and May, Suzette and I spent more time in her meditation room than in her studio. I'd trudge down her basement stairs, ready to help with some project, but she'd grow tired after only thirty minutes of painting or mold-making. Then she'd get up and limp into the adjacent room, and I'd follow her.

I spent some of the most enchanted hours of my life in that messy little room. We'd sit together at her velvet-shrouded table in the flickering candlelight, Suzette on the battered folding chair, me on the broken-down armchair. I'd listen with rapt attention as, in hushed tones, she'd talk about spiritual ideas I'd never heard of. She'd tell me otherworldly stories about her years in California, experiences with psychics, mediums, healers, and a Native American shaman. Then we'd spend half an hour in blissful meditation. With our combined focus, it always seemed as if we were on the verge of breaking through the veil that separated us from the world of the spirit, that at any moment, we'd glimpse the breathtaking wonders of the other side.

While Suzette's speech and behavior were unrelentingly irreverent, she professed a profound faith in God. When love in the earthly realm eluded her, she turned to the realm of the supernatural for solace. She'd tell me about the spirit guides who roamed her house, a wolf and an Indian chief, and she'd take comfort in knowing her helpers were nearby. "I see them out of the corner of my eye, just for an instant," she'd say. "When you open yourself up to that sort of thing, Lanie, you'll be able to see your own guides."

On her bad days, when she could do little more than rest in her recliner, she'd see a snow-white bird landing in a nearby tree, or a colorful butterfly flitting past her window. She'd take these as good omens, signs that God was looking out for her.

Suzette even had lovers in the spirit world, ready to do the job when mortal men failed her. They'd appear to her in dreams, telling her their exotic names. The next morning, she'd call to tell me about them. After a rendezvous with a spirit lover, she'd be content for several days, more satisfied with the ordinary life she shared with her lackluster husband.

After several months of meditating with Suzette, I began noticing a change in my massage practice. While giving a massage, I'd find myself slipping into a trance-like state similar to the one I experienced while meditating. I also noticed that my clients were sinking into deeper states of relaxation.

"You keep getting better and better, Elaine," one man told me. My business began to grow, and people complained about not being able to get an appointment when they wanted one.

Occasionally, Nana came in for a massage, and even she commented on the change. "Elaine," she said, "I've been to every massage therapist in Nashville. There's no doubt about it, you're the best."

I told Suzette about the changes in my practice. "That's because of your energy," she said. "Meditating is purifying your energy, and that's why your touch feels so good to your clients."

"How do you know about energy?" I asked her.

"From that woman in California," she responded, "the

one who taught me about the tarot cards. She was a psychic and an energy healer."

Even though I didn't fully understand what Suzette was talking about, I knew that what was happening in my practice was important.

From time to time, Suzette would ask, "Lanie, will you give me a free massage?" I'd always consent to her request, as I knew she couldn't afford to pay for my services.

The first time she came for an appointment, I gave her a tour of my house, although she declined mounting the steps to my upstairs bedroom. "What a sweet little place you have here, Lanie," she said as she gazed around my small kitchen and living room. "I love it. I pray that nothing ugly will ever enter your home to disturb your peace."

Whenever I'd work on her, I'd sensed her deep fatigue. It felt like her body was giving up. Once after a massage session, I was alarmed to see tears running down her face.

"What's wrong?" I asked.

"Just remembering things," she said as she wiped her eyes with a tissue. "Times when my body was treated hatefully. Your beautiful touch helps me face those memories and let them go. Thank you, Lanie. You're a true healer."

In June, I received a call from another massage therapist in town. "There's a big corporation in Columbus that's starting a wellness program for their employees," she told me. "Next Saturday, they're sponsoring a health fair. I was going to set up a booth representing my business, but something came up and I can't make it. I wondered if you'd go in my place."

"What would that involve?" I asked.

"Just set up your table and give people ten-minute

massages. It'll be an opportunity to pass out your cards and drum up more business."

"I don't need any more clients," I said. But I agreed to go anyway.

The wellness fair turned out to be a huge event, with representation from all sorts of disciplines in the field of alternative health: chiropractors, acupuncturists, Reiki masters, nutritionists, music therapists, aroma therapists, naturopaths, and more. Unfortunately, I didn't have much opportunity to explore, as I served an endless line of people waiting for their free massages.

Toward the end of the day, a young man came for a massage, a short, stocky fellow with a neat little goatee and long, dark hair pulled back into a ponytail. I registered little else about him, as I was exhausted, and the thirty people I'd already worked on had blurred together in my mind.

But my eyes popped wide open when he got off my table and said, "That was wonderful. You have such nice energy." I'd never heard anyone other than Suzette apply the term *energy* to my work.

"Thank you," he said. He picked up one of my business cards and walked away.

I breathed a sigh of relief when I saw the people around me taking down their displays. As I folded up my portable table and slipped it into its carrying case, I wondered why I'd agreed to spend a Saturday exhausting myself instead of relaxing.

I struggled wearily toward the exit door, trying to juggle the unwieldy table and a bag of linens. Suddenly, the goateed man was at my side. "Let me help," he said as he lifted the heavy table off my shoulder. "You've given to people all day long. Now, you need someone to give to you."

Gratefully, I allowed him to carry the table to my car. When I opened the trunk, he heaved it inside. Then he extended his hand and said, "I'm Aaron Matthews."

"I'm Elaine Greene," I said.

"I'd ask you to go someplace and have a drink with me, but you look beat. You should probably go home and rest."

His sensitivity astounded me. "You're right," I said.

"Can I call you some time?"

"I suppose so."

"If that would be okay," he blurted out apologetically. "Unless you're with someone else. I'm not trying to intrude on anything."

"No," I said. "I'm completely on my own."

"Then I'll call you, Elaine. Thanks again for the massage. Have a nice evening."

Stunned by his exhibition of kindness and thoughtfulness, I stood by my car watching Aaron Matthews walk away. "Who the heck is this guy?" I whispered to myself. "Where on earth did he come from?"

He seemed to be the polar opposite of the egotistical and unstable man who'd so recently terrorized my life. Still, I told myself to be cautious about allowing this new guy into my personal world.

CHAPTER 18

I soon discovered that I didn't need to worry about Aaron Matthews pushing himself into my life. When it came to relationships, he seemed to be even more cautious than I was.

He called me Tuesday evening, three days after we met at the wellness fair. During our brief conversation, he informed me that most of his life, he'd lived in Ann Arbor, Michigan. He'd graduated from the University of Michigan with a degree in art, specializing in photography. He now lived in Columbus and worked as a photographer for the Columbus newspaper, *The Republic*.

"It's not easy getting photography jobs," he told me. "Up in Michigan, I tried to make a living doing freelance photography: weddings, parties, events like that. And I was always broke. So when I got the job offer in Columbus, I jumped on it, even though it meant relocating the family to another state."

What the heck? I wondered. *Is this guy married?* "You have a family?" I asked.

"I guess that didn't sound right," he said. "I was married then. But don't worry, I'm divorced now."

"Do you have children?"

"One daughter. Her name is Eden."

We talked only a few minutes before he said, "I'm sorry, Elaine, I need to go. I always call Eden right around her bedtime. Her mother says hearing my voice helps her settle down and go to sleep."

"How old is Eden?" I asked.

"Eight," he replied. "It sounds like I baby her, doesn't it?"

It seemed to me that was exactly what he was doing, but I said, "I can't be the judge of that."

"I'd like to get together with you sometime. But it can't be this weekend, because I'll have Eden. Maybe the following weekend?"

"We'll see," I said. "Give me a call when you're free." I told myself not to get excited about this man, that I didn't care whether our first date was next week, next month, or next year.

The following Tuesday evening, I ran some sculptures over to Suzette's house. When I got home, I discovered that Aaron had left a message on my answering machine. Since it was quite late and I had an early client the next morning, I decided to wait to return his call until the next evening.

Aaron seemed pleased to hear from me. "I'm glad you called, Elaine, but I can't talk now. Eden is here. She's with me every Wednesday evening and every other weekend. Can we talk tomorrow night?"

"That's fine," I said. "I'll let you call me." I hung up the phone wondering why this man was trying so hard to connect with me when he clearly didn't have the time to do so.

But he did call the next evening, and this time, we talked for an hour, sharing more details of our lives. He was quite surprised to learn that before I'd begun my massage therapy career, I'd also been an art major.

"I just wasn't cut out for it," I told him.

"Well, as far as I'm concerned," he said, "you're right on track with your life's purpose in being a massage therapist. You're really good at it, and like I told you, you have nice energy. I've been to quite a few different massage therapists, and sometimes their energy is so off-putting, I don't even like having them touch me."

"It's funny that you keep mentioning energy," I said. Then I told him about my work with Suzette, and how she'd introduced me to meditation. "She says I'm a natural at it. I don't know about that, but I do know I love it. It helps me stay calm and focused."

"Wow!" Aaron exclaimed. "We have so much in common, the artistic side and the spiritual side."

"Do you meditate, too?" I asked.

"Yes, I do."

"How did you get into it?"

"That's a long story. Do you have time to hear it?"

"Sure," I said, genuinely curious.

Then he told me that up until his mid-twenties, he'd never given any thought to spirituality. "I was just your average young person, drinking, partying, following every stupid, self-centered whim I had. And I ended up getting a girl pregnant."

He and Diana hadn't had a serious relationship, but he stuck with her during the pregnancy and was there for the birth of their daughter. And both of them were devastated when their child was born with spina bifida.

"I sat for hours watching my daughter lying in her little incubator," he said. "She was so beautiful, but so tiny and fragile. During that time, my life changed completely. I did a total turnaround in my thoughts about myself and what I wanted out of life. I knew the world wasn't going to be an easy place for my daughter, and that it was my responsibility to take care of her and protect her. I knew without a doubt what my priority needed to be."

He and Diana had gotten married, because it had seemed like that would make it easier for them to take care of their special-needs child. "The best part of my life has been the time I've spent with Eden," he said. "She's stimulated my desire to understand my higher self."

He told me he'd begun studying different spiritual traditions, which led him to becoming involved with a meditation group in Ann Arbor. "So that's where I learned all about meditation," he said, "and the energy system and the chakras. Have you done any work with the chakras?"

"No," I said. "I've never heard of chakras."

"I'll have to show you sometime. I've learned to do energy healing with the chakras. I do energy healing on Eden every time she's with me."

But I had another topic in mind that interested me more than chakras. "Why did you get divorced?" I asked.

"I hate to admit this," he said. "It was because of my selfishness. My wife never developed an interest in my meditation group, and I ended up spending a lot of time there without her. After we moved to Columbus, I was still running up to Michigan every couple of months for the group's weekend trainings. Diana hated that. She felt like I was abandoning her and Eden. I thought I was doing something good for myself, but I guess it wasn't good for our family.

"Eden had gone through a lot of surgeries, and I'd been there for all of them. She had another one coming up, just a minor procedure, and it conflicted with some training I wanted to attend at the group. I decided it was more important to be at the training than with my child. And Eden nearly died during that surgery. Diana went through that horrible experience all alone, while I was up there in Michigan doing my own thing.

"I felt terrible about what I'd done, and I vowed I'd never again put anyone or anything above my child's wellbeing. I knew right then and there that my highest purpose in life was being Eden's father.

"But Diana couldn't get over my having abandoned her during that time. She said she'd completely lost trust in me, and she ended up filing for divorce. So now I have to do the best I can with being a part-time father."

"Does your ex-wife live around here?" I asked.

"Yes," he said. "She manages a beauty salon here in Columbus. We get along pretty well now. We're friends, and we cooperate when it comes to Eden. I don't think Diana has any reason to complain about me now."

When I hung up the phone, I wondered about this honest, sensitive, deep-thinking man who was so unlike any other guy I'd ever met. He didn't possess charisma or stunning good looks, and women wouldn't fall all over themselves to date him like they would Jesse Jordan. Yet, I felt drawn to him in a way that I didn't understand.

"That little Eden's a lucky child," Suzette observed when I told her about my conversations with Aaron. "Not many children have such a dedicated father. I would've given anything for a dad who loved me like that."

Later, she asked, "When's he going to have time to date you?"

"I don't know," I said.

"Has he actually asked you out?"

"Not yet," I admitted.

CHAPTER 19

Aaron called me a week later, in the middle of a July thunderstorm. "I know this is short notice," he said, "but do you have any free time tomorrow afternoon? I was scheduled to photograph an anniversary party, but they cancelled it."

He sighed. "I was counting on that money. So I'm pretty broke. I thought maybe we could do something low-budget. This storm's supposed to cool things off, so the weather should be perfect tomorrow. Would you be up for a hike in Brown County State Park?"

"Sure," I said.

"I've lived in the area for four years now," he continued, "and I've never been on any of the trails in the park. That's a shame, isn't it? I guess you'll have to be my tour guide. How about if we meet at the West Gatehouse at 1:00?"

"Are you up for a rugged hike?" Aaron asked the next afternoon as we studied the trail map we'd picked up at the park's gatehouse. "I feel like I could use a good workout."

"Absolutely," I said. "Let's head toward Trail 5." I traced the trail's route on the map with my finger. "See? It goes down through Ogle Hollow Nature Preserve."

As we made our way down the preserve's rugged slope, Aaron listened with appreciation as I pointed out the different species of southern Indiana trees: redbud, dogwood, pawpaw, spicebush, ironwood, and musclewood.

In the middle of my oratory, I slipped on a loose rock and slid a ways down the slope on my bottom. Aaron rushed to me, reaching out a hand to help me up. "Are you okay?" he asked, alarmed.

Laughing, I brushed the dirt off the seat of my blue jeans,

while Aaron brushed off my shoulders and picked a few twigs out of my hair.

"Well, that was a jolt," I said. Then we both laughed, and I thought about how much I enjoyed the company of this gentle, easy-going man.

A few minutes later, when I pointed out the rare yellowwood trees, Aaron said, "This is so amazing! I love being in nature. But I don't get to do a lot of serious hiking like this. It isn't something I can share with my daughter. She wouldn't make it ten feet with her crutches on a trail like this, and with her wheelchair, we'd need a smooth paved path."

I was surprised when I realized I was clenching my jaws in irritation. *You're here with me,* I wanted to tell him. *This is my time, not Eden's. Why can't you just enjoy this hike with me?*

We found a bench at the end of our rugged trail, where it intersected with the easier Trail 4. With relief, we sat down to catch our breath. Aaron took my hand and gently ran his index finger over the lines in my palm. "You have beautiful hands," he said. Then he interlaced his fingers with mine. "It's so nice to be close to someone. Thanks for sharing this time with me."

"You're welcome," I said. I felt a sudden urge to rest my head against his shoulder, but just then, his cell phone rang. He dropped my hand, grabbed the phone out of his pocket, and said, "I've got to take this. It's Eden's mother."

I could hear the woman's frustrated voice barking on the other end of the line. Aaron listened patiently, a worried expression on his face. "Let me talk to her," he finally said. He looked sideways at me and whispered, "She's having problems with Eden."

Then he got up and wandered away, and I could hear the placating tone in his voice as he tried to cajole his daughter into a more cooperative frame of mind. "Will you promise to be good for Mommy?" he asked as he finished up the conversation. "I'll call you this evening. I love you, baby."

Then he walked back to where I was sitting and said, "I guess we'd better go now." We spoke little as we headed back toward the gatehouse on Trail 4. Aaron seemed tense and preoccupied.

I didn't see Aaron for another month. He called me once or twice a week, each time apologizing for having no time to spend with me. Either it was his weekend with his daughter, or he had some freelance photography job lined up.

Once, I timidly suggested that he, Eden, and I could do something together. "I don't think that's a good idea," he said hurriedly. "I don't want Eden to think she has to compete with someone else for my attention."

His response stunned me. After a long silence between us, Aaron said, "I realize what I just told you probably made you feel second-rate. I want you to know I do care about you."

"Aaron," I said, "why do you bother to call me? You don't have time for me."

"I'm so sorry," he said. "I really like you, and I hope that someday, things will work out between us."

I hung up the phone, determined to put Aaron out of my mind. *This isn't going anywhere,* I told myself. *Let it go, Elaine.*

But three days later, he called me again. "Are you free Saturday night?" he asked, excitement in his voice. "I promise you this will be our time. I got a call for a freelance job, but I turned it down. I won't have Eden, and I'll tell Diana not to interrupt us."

That Saturday evening, Aaron came to my home bringing carryout food for dinner. While we ate, he admired the sculpting projects sitting on my kitchen table. Suzette had asked me to mold the figures from the song, *The Twelve Days of Christmas,* and I'd already completed the partridge, the turtledoves, and the French hens.

"You're quite talented," he observed. "I have a hard time believing you couldn't make it as an art student."

After we finished eating, I showed him my treatment room. As we stood together, he put his arm around me. "This is a nice space," he said. "I like the energy in here."

Being so close to Aaron felt wonderful. All I wanted to do was to snuggle up to him, to melt into him. "Thank you," I said, trying to maintain a fragment of self-control. In spite of the frustration of the previous weeks, I couldn't keep myself from being powerfully drawn to him again. It was impossible for me to resist this man.

"I promised I'd tell you about the chakras," he said. "Maybe this would be a good time. Want to do a chakra meditation with me?"

He helped me move my massage table to one side of the room. Then, following his instruction, I sat cross-legged on the floor facing him. "The chakras are the energy centers of the body," he informed me. He proceeded to explain the colors and sounds associated with each one.

Then he moved into a guided meditation that incorporated all the chakras, beginning with the root chakra and moving up through the sacral, solar plexus, heart, throat, brow, and crown chakras. His soothing voice mesmerized me, and as our focus moved up the body, I felt increasingly peaceful. By the time we reached the crown chakra, I felt so light and airy that it seemed as if my body had dissolved into a mist.

I opened my eyes and looked at Aaron sitting across from me. He appeared blissful, radiant. I had the odd perception that there was no separation between us, that we were one being.

He opened his eyes and smiled at me. Then he slowly stood up and held out his hand to help me to my feet. I glided into his arms, and he began to kiss me ever so sweetly on my face, my neck, and my lips.

"Take me to your bedroom," he whispered.

Our lovemaking was nothing like the boring copulation I'd shared with my husband. It felt exquisite, sacred, an inevitable outcome of the spiritual intimacy we'd shared. Aaron and I were truly one.

When Aaron left my home that evening, I was convinced that our destiny as soul mates had been established, that our lovemaking had carried our budding relationship to a new level. I smiled when I thought about Suzette's tarot card prediction. My encounter with Jesse Jordan had been a fluke. Surely, this was the real thing.

I'd fallen hard for Aaron Matthews, so hard that the intensity of my feelings frightened me. I wanted his loving attention every moment of every day. I wanted him all to myself. I wanted to devour him.

CHAPTER 20

Aaron called me the next day, and our conversation was sweet and intimate. When we said goodbye, I told him I missed him. "I miss you, too, Elaine," he sighed. "I hope we can see each other soon."

But days passed before Aaron called me again. My heart longed for him. My body ached for his touch. I'd felt alone most of my life, and I'd grown accustomed to that. But this loneliness for my new lover felt unbearable. Like Eden, I wanted to hear his voice every night before I fell asleep, and I resented the child who had everything I didn't have.

When I finally heard from Aaron, he informed me that Eden had developed an infection and had been hospitalized. As it turned out, the infection was easily treated with antibiotics, and she was released from the hospital after only two days. But the whole thing worried Aaron terribly.

I tried to offer him words of encouragement, and he thanked me, but I could tell he was slipping away from me. And I began to hate the little girl who inevitably won the competition for his attention, who had so much more than I ever had when I was a child. She'd been welcomed into the world by two doting parents and was being raised as if she was the center of the universe. I'd grown up believing that I was nothing more than the byproduct of my mother's tragic misstep, and watching Aaron's relationship with his spoiled daughter pushed every button I had about feeling second-rate.

One evening in September, after I hadn't heard from Aaron for several days, I couldn't stand the loneliness any longer. I picked up the phone and called him.

"I can't talk now, Elaine," he said. "Eden is with me." I could hear a hint of irritation in his voice, and I realized I'd completely forgotten that Wednesday evening was his time with his daughter.

I hung up the phone and threw myself across my bed, too stung to even cry. *You're turning into a stalker like Jesse Jordan,* I berated myself. *Let him go, Elaine. You've got to let this man go.*

I got up and wandered out to the kitchen, where my gaze fell on the *Twelve Days of Christmas* figurines sitting on my table. I realized I'd been so pre-occupied with my feelings about Aaron that I hadn't touched my sculpting for several weeks. I sat down and began to work on the four calling birds, and the feel of cool clay under my fingertips began to soothe my nerves. After half an hour of work, I felt exhausted, so I went to bed.

Around 10:30, the phone rang, waking me from a sound sleep. It was Aaron. "I didn't want you to think I don't want to talk to you," he said.

"Well, I'm beginning to wonder." My voice sounded harsher than I wanted it to. "In the past two months, we've seen each other exactly twice. Face it, Aaron. You don't have time for me." Then I embarrassed myself by adding in a petulant tone, "I don't think you even care about me."

"Elaine, I don't want you to feel that way," he said. "If I made you feel like I don't care, then I'm really sorry. I care a lot about you, I really do."

The next evening, he called again, sounding excited. "I have an idea, Elaine. There's something coming up at my meditation group in Michigan two weeks from this weekend. It's an important ceremony, one of the biggest events of the year. I plan to go."

"Well, that's nice," I said, feeling rather indifferent.

"Would you like to come with me? I think you'd enjoy it, and you'd meet some really interesting people. We could take in part of the ceremony, and then travel on to the west coast of Michigan. We could hike along the beaches and check out a few little towns: Saint Joseph, South Haven, Saugatuck. I don't have money for motel rooms, but I can borrow some camping gear from a friend. I know all the good camping sites. What do you think, Elaine?"

I could hardly believe what I'd heard him say. "Really? You'd take me with you?"

"Absolutely! Wanna do it?"

"Of course!" I said.

For the next two weeks, I savored sweet anticipation. Since my divorce from Kevin, I hadn't traveled any farther than the forty-five minute drive to Indianapolis. Not only did I look forward to the adventure with Aaron, I envisioned us getting closer, solidifying the tenuous bond of our relationship. He was ready to take me into his personal world, to introduce me to people who were important to him. Surely, that signified that I was about to earn a more important spot in his life.

I canceled all my appointments for the Monday following our scheduled trip, allowing for the long weekend Aaron had proposed. I even drove to the FairOaks mall in Columbus to buy jeans, shirts, and boots suitable for camping and hiking.

When Aaron called the Thursday evening before the Saturday we were scheduled to leave, I heard dejection in his voice, and I immediately knew the plans for our dream weekend had been dashed to pieces.

"I can't believe I have to tell you this, Elaine," he said. "We have to cancel our trip."

"You've got to be kidding me!" I exclaimed.

"No, unfortunately, I'm not. Diana just called me. Her aunt died, and she needs to fly to Florida for the funeral. She asked me to take Eden for the weekend. I'm so sorry, but I don't have any other choice."

Tears began coursing down my cheeks. "Okay," I whispered.

"Please forgive me, Elaine," he pleaded. "I'll do everything I can to make it up to you. I promise."

"We'll see," I said before hanging up the phone.

After an hour of distraught sobbing, I called Suzette. "Can I come over Saturday and help you with something?"

"I thought you had plans with your man," she said.

"I did have plans. I don't anymore."

"Then come on over, honey. I'm no substitute for Aaron, but at least we can keep each other company."

Two days later, when I walked down the narrow staircase to Suzette's studio, I saw that she'd molded a batch of resin cows from the first sculpture I'd created almost a year ago.

"I'm making more of those old-fashioned pull toys," she told me. "They're selling pretty well. I owe you a check. Remind me before you go."

As I painted the white basecoat on the figurines, tears ran down my cheeks. Suzette eyed me with concern. When a tear fell on a cow, making the wet paint run, she said, "For Heaven's sake, Lanie, would you put down your paintbrush and talk to me? You're not going to get anything done like this."

So I pushed aside the cow and the bottle of paint, and between sobs, I recounted the details of my canceled plans. "I was looking forward to that trip more than I've looked forward to anything in my entire life. Aaron was excited about it, too. But his daughter gets in the way of everything."

"The man's only doing what he needs to do," Suzette observed as she carefully painted a black spot on a cow's back. "You've got to give him credit for that. And if you're going to be with him, you need to cut him slack about his daughter. He's in a tough situation, you know."

She set the cow aside to dry, and then looked at me sternly. "Lanie, you've got to realize that if you want to be Aaron's girlfriend, you'll always take second place to that child. He told you his daughter comes first, didn't he?"

I nodded.

"He was telling you the truth. Why would you expect anything different?"

"You're right," I mumbled. "I know you're right. I guess I'll just have to be more patient."

A few minutes later, Suzette sighed heavily, furrowing her brow as if deep in thought. "I'm going to tell you something, Lanie," she said, "and I don't want you to take offense. I just want you to think about what I'm saying." She eyed me over the top of her bifocals, as if assessing my readiness to take in the wisdom she was about to impart.

"What?" I sniffled.

She folded her arms on the table and leaned toward me. "Honey, you weren't raised with enough love. And because of that, you're going to be a little bit needy in a relationship. You're going to want your man to make up for everything you didn't have when you were a child."

I opened my mouth to protest, but she held up a hand to stop me. “I’m not putting you down. I’m just saying the way it is. I’m that way, too, you know. I’ll admit it, when it comes to needing love and attention, I’m a bottomless pit. Aaron might be a wonderful person, but there’s no room for you at the top of his list. Maybe you need a man who can put you first.”

CHAPTER 21

I didn't have much to do that following Monday, as I'd canceled all my massage appointments in anticipation of the trip. So I spent most of the morning sitting at my kitchen table, sculpting.

This time, my project wasn't one commissioned by Suzette. I decided to let my imagination run free, to see what ideas came to me on my own. For awhile, I did nothing but knead the clay, rolling it, flattening it, and forming it into a ball again. Then I began to shape a figure of a woman, a beautiful, graceful woman, sitting with her head bowed, her eyes downcast. I took the fine tip of one of my sculpting tools and etched tears on her face. I imagined what Suzette would say about the sculpture: "That's good, Lanie. You're expressing your feelings through your art."

The work carried me into another world, where nothing existed but the weeping woman and me. I felt strangely close to her, as if she and I knew each other on a deep level, and the intimacy comforted me. But then the ringing of the telephone jolted me back into the here and now.

It was Aaron. I suddenly realized that he, too, was free, as he'd also cleared his schedule for the trip. I wondered if he wanted to spend the day with me, and for a moment, I envisioned us back in each other's arms, making passionate love like we had weeks earlier.

"Can I come over for a few minutes, Elaine?" he asked. The nervousness in his voice immediately dispelled my fantasy.

When he arrived twenty minutes later, I invited him to sit down and talk. But he remained standing by the door, shifting his weight from one foot to the other. "I don't know how to say this, Elaine," he finally blurted out. "So I'll just cut to the chase. We can't see each other anymore."

I wasn't completely surprised by his announcement. Still, his words landed with a heavy thud in my heart. "Why not?" I asked.

He looked so uncomfortable that I almost felt sorry for him. "Diana and I are . . . are working on getting back together," he stammered. "We figured it would be best for Eden if we tried living together again. Shuffling her back and forth puts a lot of strain on her."

I looked down, shaking my head, feeling completely fed up and disgusted with Aaron's unreasonable preoccupation with his child. Then I looked up and met his gaze. "How long have the two of you been talking about this?"

He hung his head. "About a month."

"The same time you were planning a trip with me?"

He nodded, his face contorted in pain. "I was confused, Elaine. I didn't know what I wanted."

Anger boiled inside me, threatening to erupt in a volcanic explosion. "Why did you start things with me if you're still involved with Diana? Why did you put me through this?"

"I can't say that I was involved with Diana. I'm not in love with her, Elaine. I'm actually more attracted to you. But I'm hoping she and I can kindle something."

"So you're just trying to do the right thing," I said.

Apparently, he didn't pick up on the sarcasm in my voice. "Yes. Thank you for understanding that."

I wanted to scream at him that I didn't understand. I wanted to rant about what an idiot he was for not insisting on a life of his own, what a jerk he was for leading me on like he did. But the poor man's face told me he was already berating himself more mercilessly than I ever could.

"Just go, Aaron," I said, trying to hold back my tears. "Go on, get out of here."

"I hate myself for what I put you through," he whimpered as I closed the door in his face. "I'm really not a guy who messes with other people's feelings."

After Aaron pulled out of my driveway, I could think of only one thing to do. I got in my car and drove to Helmsburg. When Suzette found me weeping on her doorstep, she sat me down on her sofa and gathered me in her arms.

"Let me guess," she said. "He broke up with you." As she held me, she began praying over me. "Dear Lord, this precious child of yours is in pain. Right now, she doesn't feel lovable, because some jerk treated her like crap. Please heal her broken heart. Let her know that she deserves love, and that someday, she'll find the love she needs."

Her prayer triggered uncontrollable sobbing on my part. "I thought Aaron was the one," I blubbered. "The one your tarot cards predicted."

"Shhh," she said as she rocked me and patted my back. Then she continued her prayer. "Lord, help your precious child remember that she deserves better than that stupid creep who just dumped her. Forgive the son-of-a-bitch for being too ignorant to know that he just threw away the best thing that ever happened to him."

I almost laughed through my tears.

Suzette continued to hold me until my sobs subsided. Then she said, "Let's go downstairs, Lanie."

I figured she thought doing a little painting would settle my nerves. But she led me through her studio and on into her meditation room. There, she coached me through the basics, as she had the first time we meditated together. "Okay, Lanie, pay attention to your posture. You need to sit up straighter than that. Now breathe as deeply as you can. I know it's hard when you're upset. Just ease into it."

Slowly, my agitation subsided, leaving me feeling exhausted and completely empty. As I listened to Suzette's labored breathing on the other side of the velvet-shrouded table, the familiar sound comforted me. My own breathing began keeping pace with hers.

Suddenly, Suzette broke the deep stillness in the room when she murmured, "I sense another presence with us."

My eyes popped open. "Huh?"

"Shhh," she cautioned. "Let me concentrate."

A moment later, she said, "It's someone for you, Lanie. Someone from the other side."

"The other side?"

"Someone who died, silly."

What on earth is she talking about? I wondered. But I forced myself to remain quiet.

After a minute of silence, Suzette said, "It's a male. He's from the generation older than you, like a father figure. I get the impression of dark hair and dark eyes. Do you know who that might be?"

My heart pounded with excitement. Still, I remained dubious. Suzette's tarot card prediction had proven to be utterly worthless. It had done nothing other than confuse me and set me up for disappointment. I told myself not to get caught up in her current flight of fancy.

But I played along anyway. "My dad? Could it be my dad?"

"Yes," she said. "I'm sure it is. He's offering you a bouquet of pink roses, a sign of his love."

"I don't like pink," I said. "At least not pale pink. I like hot pink."

"He says he knows that. The roses are bright pink."

In spite of my reservations, I leaned forward, captivated. "What else does he say?"

Suzette held up a finger to silence me. She looked dazed and distant. "He's telling you to believe in yourself."

"Oh." I sat back in my chair, disappointed with the vague information.

"Mostly, he's telling you that he loves you. It seems like a long time ago, there was a question about that. He's insistent. He wants you to know that he loves you."

My mind flashed back to when I was a tiny child. "I know what he means," I said. "When I was four, I asked my mother if my daddy loved me. She told me he didn't have a chance to love me, because he died before I was born."

Suzette smiled. "He says that doesn't matter. He says that even if you never knew him, he's known you, and that he's always loved you."

"Can I ask him questions?"

Suzette shook her head. "He seems to be pulling back. Sorry, Lanie, he's gone now."

For a full five minutes, we sat in silence. Suzette's eyes remained closed, and I sensed she was far away, still in another reality. I gazed at her face in the flickering candlelight, trying to make sense of the jolting experiences I'd had that day, first with Aaron, and then, supposedly, with my father.

Finally, Suzette opened her eyes and looked at me pointedly, as if trying to ascertain how I'd responded to our strange adventure.

"Do you do this often?" I asked.

"Do what often?"

"Talk with dead people."

"Not often," she said. "It just happens once in awhile."

"How do you do it?"

She yawned, and then stretched her neck and her arms as if she'd just woken up from a sound sleep. "I don't do anything. They just come to me."

"Did my father say anything else?"

She stood up, ready to leave the room. "Lanie, I've already told you everything he communicated to me. I'm tired. I need to lay down now."

I was almost home when I heard the warning beep of my gas gage. I glanced down and saw that the red pointer was on empty.

"Yikes!" I said to myself. "I almost ran out of gas!" So instead of pulling into my driveway, I headed on down to the Shell station on Van Buren Street in Nashville.

When I went inside to pay for my gas, I spotted a container of silk roses sitting on the counter. Most of them were red, and a few were white. One was bright pink.

Without thinking, I plucked it out of the container. "I'll take this, too," I told the cashier.

CHAPTER 22

After my tumultuous chapter with Aaron finally came to a close, I returned to my sculpting with renewed interest. While I worked on finishing Suzette's *Twelve Days of Christmas* figurines, my thoughts repeatedly turned to our last session in her meditation room. In spite of my determination to remain skeptical, the more I contemplated the supposed encounter with my father, the more excited I became.

I desperately hoped he'd appear to Suzette again. I told myself he had to, because I had so many things I needed to ask him. While I sat at my kitchen table sculpting, I kept a pen and paper at hand to jot down questions as they came to me: *What part of Kentucky did you come from? How many brothers and sisters did you have? What did your parents do for a living? What did you enjoy doing as a child? What were you good at? What were your hopes and dreams for your future? What made you decide to leave Kentucky and move to Indiana? Did you love my mother? How did you feel when you found out she was pregnant with me? Were you excited about being a father?*

I went so far as to rehearse my questions out loud, speaking to my father as if he was right there in the room with me. Then I felt a little embarrassed, telling myself I was getting carried away. Nevertheless, I carefully tucked the list into my handbag, preparing myself for the event of another meditation room visit.

The next time I knocked on the Perrys' front door, Eldon was the one who answered it. "Come on in, Lanie," he said. "Suzette's taking a nap, but she'll probably be up soon.

As I was holding a large box containing the *Twelve Days of Christmas* figurines, he couldn't wrap me in a hug like he usually did. But he slipped an arm around my shoulders and escorted me to the dining room. "Let me see what you've brought."

I set the box on the table and pulled out one piece at a time, proudly announcing its name. "This is the partridge. The turtle doves. The French hens. The calling birds. The five golden rings."

Eldon exclaimed over each one, repeatedly telling me, "You're so good, Lanie."

Just as I set the last piece on the table, Suzette shuffled out of her bedroom, buttoning up her flimsy housecoat as if she'd just thrown it on. Her frizzy hair was standing on end, and she looked haggard, her face grim.

Without saying a word, she sat down at the table and picked up each of the figures in turn. "Aren't they good?" Eldon said.

Suzette nodded slowly as she examined the piper and the drummer. "These are excellent. Perfect. I can't keep up with you anymore, Lanie. I have no idea when I'll get around to molding these."

She sighed deeply as she heaved herself out of her chair. "Well, let's go downstairs and see if we can get something done."

As I followed her down the narrow staircase, I couldn't contain my impatience, and I blurted out, "Can we talk to my father again today?"

Suzette remained silent while she negotiated the last few treacherous steps. When she reached the bottom, she turned around to look at me, and I saw anger on her face. "I already told you," she snapped. "I can't do this just because you want it done. This kind of thing happens when it happens, and I don't have any control over it."

She began randomly shoving things around on her table. "Besides, Lanie, you can't just use me like that. I don't think you came over here today to spend time with me. You just wanted what you could get out of me."

I'd known Suzette for over a year, and I was used to her bluntness and her grumpy moods. But this time, her sharp reproach hurt me deeply.

"I'm sorry," I whispered.

Suzette walked over to a shelf and began bringing handfuls of figurines to the table. I saw that she'd molded the nativity figures I'd sculpted the previous year.

"I've made up my mind," she said, her voice suddenly cheerful. "One way or the other, I'm going to have these ready to sell this holiday season. I plan to put them in the shop in Nashville right after Thanksgiving, so I've got about six or seven weeks to get them done. Eldon's building little wooden stables for me in the garage. You should see them. They're really cute."

She told me the colors of the basecoats she wanted on the different figures, and I meekly followed her instructions. But I was still feeling stung by her outburst. I'd never before snapped back at Suzette when she snapped at me, and I wondered whether I could get away with being as cranky as she was.

As she painted purple robes on a row of figures of the Virgin Mary, Suzette eyed me from time to time, seemingly worried about my silence. Finally, she said, "I hope you know I still love you, Lanie."

I nodded while continuing to paint a drab brown cloak on the figure of a shepherd.

Then, as if nothing at all had happened between us, Suzette changed the subject. "I went to a family gathering at my brother Oscar's house last weekend. It was a birthday party for my brother Marvin. All my brothers were there. I don't know why I even bothered to go. Those sons-of-bitches are as mean as ever. The only time they pay attention to me is when they're picking on me."

Her voice took on the tone of a little girl who'd had her tender feelings wounded. "They started making fun of what I do. When I mentioned something about my business, my brother Harold got a smirk on his ugly old face and said, 'It's not a business if you aren't making any money.'"

She shook her head in disgust. "I'm not stupid, Lanie, even though they think I am. I know I don't make a lot of money off my crafts, and I know I don't pay you very much for what you do." She set down the figure she was painting and made a sweeping gesture with her hand. "They don't understand that this isn't all about money. Those knuckleheads don't realize that a person could do something just because their heart and soul is in it."

I suddenly felt sorry for her, and in spite of my intention to continue my sulk, I felt the urge to comfort her. "You shouldn't pay attention to those jerks," I said. "They don't know what they're talking about."

She sighed deeply. "I know that, Lanie. You'd think I'd get that through this thick head of mine, but I don't. What they say still hurts me." She wiped a tear with the back of her paint-splattered hand, leaving a purple smudge on her cheek.

We painted our figurines in silence for awhile, and the quiet rhythm of our work lulled me into a state of drowsiness. All of a sudden, Suzette said, "Oh my God, Lanie, I just saw your dad again!"

Her words jerked me into alertness. I stared at her, wide-eyed. "Really?"

"Yes," she said. "It was quick, just a flash. But I'm sure it was him."

"Did he say something?"

She chuckled. "No, but it seemed like he was trying to joke with you. They do that sometimes, you know. He was holding a pink rose in one hand and a seashell in the other hand."

"A seashell?" I asked. "What does that mean?"

She shrugged. "I have no idea." Then she put down her paintbrush and held up her hands, her long fingers splayed out. "It was one of those big flat shells with ridges that fan out like this."

Suddenly, the association clicked for me, and I laughed. "He's talking about the Shell gas station. When I went home two weeks ago, I bought gas at the Shell station in Nashville, and I saw some silk roses there. I bought a pink one because it reminded me of him."

Suzette grinned impishly, looking like a child with her missing tooth and the paint smudge on her face. "Your dad's teasing you, Lanie. He's such a nut!"

"What do you want me to work on next?" I asked Suzette as I stood in her living room, ready to leave.

"I have an idea," she said. "I won't have time to mold anything else until after the holidays, but if you want to start on it now, you can go ahead."

"What is it?"

"You know how much people love their pets. Well, I'm thinking they might buy figurines that look like their own dogs and cats. I was thinking we could start a line of sculptures of the different dog breeds."

"That's sounds like a great idea," I said. "I could have fun with that."

She pointed to her own dog sleeping on the sofa. "Start with a Chihuahua. Start with Daisy."

"Okay," I agreed. "Next time I come, I'll bring my camera and take some pictures of her."

CHAPTER 23

A week later, I called Suzette on a Sunday afternoon. "Can I come over to take some pictures of Daisy?" I asked.

She was silent for so long that I wondered if the line had gone dead. "Sure, honey," she finally said. "You can come if you want to, but you need to know my nephew is here."

The coolness in her voice baffled me. Suzette had never before sounded reluctant to spend time with me.

"You mean Butch or Larry?" I asked, thinking I might prefer to postpone my visit.

"No." Her voice suddenly bubbled with enthusiasm. "It's Tommy, my real nephew. Well, he's not quite my real nephew. He's my oldest brother Oscar's stepson. I haven't seen Tommy in ten years, but God has brought him back into my life. It feels like a miracle that the two of us are together again."

Suzette had frequently spoken of her brothers: Oscar, Marvin, Everett, Floyd, and Harold. I felt like I knew all of those contemptible characters just through her colorful descriptions of them. But she'd never mentioned Tommy, and I wondered about his sudden reappearance in her life.

"We've been having such a wonderful time catching up with each other," she continued. "I used to babysit Tommy when we were kids. He's only eight years younger than I am. I always felt so sorry for him. That son-of-a-bitch Oscar used to beat the poor little guy half to death."

"Where's Tommy been all these years?" I asked.

"He's been locked up," she said glibly.

"How's come?"

"Lanie, that's nobody's business but his."

"Okay," I said, miffed.

"He's so handsome," she sighed, as if that was all that really mattered.

When I arrived at the Perrys' house an hour later, Eldon greeted me at the door with a smothering hug. "Suzette's in the basement with Tommy," he informed me. "She said to tell you to come on down."

I found Suzette seated at her molding table, her back to me. She was deeply engrossed in a conversation with a man, apparently instructing him in the art of mold-making.

"Hi, Suzette," I called.

She turned quickly and struggled to her feet. "Oh. Hi, Lanie."

Once again, the coolness in her voice puzzled me. She seemed guarded, and I could tell she wasn't happy to see me.

She gestured toward her companion. "Lanie, this is my nephew Tommy Crawford. Tommy, this is my friend Lanie Greene. She's the one I was telling you about, the one who did all these sculptures."

Tommy Crawford was a long, lean fellow in his mid-forties, with large, soulful blue eyes. He wore faded blue jeans, and the rolled-up sleeves of his flannel shirt revealed his sinewy forearms. His light brown hair straggled out from under his baseball cap and curled on the nape of his neck.

I had to admit that Suzette was right. Her nephew certainly was handsome in an untamed sort of way, a tragic, sensual figure that a woman would fall all over herself to rescue. But I could also tell he was the kind of guy a woman would later come to despise when her rehabilitation efforts yielded no results.

For a moment, I felt a pull of unhealthy attraction toward Tommy Crawford.

But only for a moment. It was my turn to be intuitive and clear-sighted, and the next instant, I saw something that Suzette couldn't see, or didn't want to see.

The picture was right there in front of me, painted in bold, harsh strokes. I could tell by the way Suzette's eyes softened when she looked at Tommy, by the sweetness in her voice when she spoke to him, that her affection for him was far more than that of a doting aunt. I knew that since Tommy wasn't a blood relative, she was allowing herself to indulge in romantic fantasies about him. She would never possess the confidence to make a blatant overture toward a younger, good-looking man, but she'd do everything she could to keep him close to her.

And I was dead certain that the only reason Tommy Crawford was sitting there in her dank, messy basement was to take advantage of those affections. I wanted to shake Suzette, to wake her up and make her see, but I knew it would be pointless.

Tommy fixed his soulful eyes on me and said, "I like what you do, Lanie."

"Thank you," I responded. "Is Suzette showing you how to make molds?"

He grinned, showing tobacco-stained teeth. "She's trying to. But I'm a slow learner."

Suzette laid a possessive hand on her nephew's shoulder. "Don't believe a word he says, Lanie. Tommy's very talented. He's an artist himself."

"Really?" I said. "What do you do, Tommy?"

"Woodworking," Suzette said, jumping in to speak for him. "He's really good at it. We've talked about how he can help with my business. He can do the stuff Eldon never gets around to doing." She rolled her eyes, shaking her head.

Her insinuation that her husband was lazy angered me. *Really, Suzette? Eldon goes to work every day while you sit at home doing your own thing. You have him at your beck and call, and that's not enough for you?*

Thick, noxious tension filled the air in the studio, hovering over the three of us, nearly choking me. I knew that whether or not Tommy was capable of doing anything productive, Suzette now viewed him, not me, as her primary partner in business. More than that, Tommy had replaced me as the central focus of her life. She was now wrapping her heart and soul around him, and there was nothing I could do but step aside. I was so jealous of Tommy Crawford that I could hardly stand to look at him.

And I sensed Suzette was also jealous, because I had momentarily diverted Tommy's attention away from her. Clearly, she didn't want to share him. Tommy's presence had most certainly disrupted the easy flow of understanding between Suzette and me.

"Let's go upstairs," she said gruffly. She led the way, and Tommy followed close behind, from time to time reaching out a hand to steady her.

Sulking, I followed at a distance, and when I reached the top of the stairs, I headed straight toward the door, eager to remove my unwelcome presence from the Perrys' home. But then I remembered what I came for, and fished my camera out of my handbag.

While I was snapping photos of Daisy, Eldon brought out his oversized Aggravation board. "Wanna play a game, Lanie?" he asked.

"I should go," I protested.

He contorted his face into a pout. "Can't you stay for just one game?"

Suddenly, I felt sorry for Suzette's unsuspecting husband, and I decided to humor him. So I sat down with him, Suzette, and Tommy at the dining room table for a game of Aggravation.

Eldon fawned over me like he usually did. Suzette ignored her husband, angling her body away from him and toward her nephew, whom she sweetly schooled in the rules of the game. "No, no, Tommy, you can't do that," she'd say, playfully smacking his hand.

Like Eldon's son Kenneth had been a year earlier, Tommy was quiet throughout the game. But while Kenneth's silence had reflected cool indifference verging on boredom, Tommy's silence blanketed an inner well of simmering agitation. In spite of the autumn chill in the room, beads of perspiration stood out on his forehead and across the bridge of his nose, and his hands shook every time he reached out to move one of his marbles. I wondered whether he was suffering from some type of illness.

CHAPTER 24

I ended up sculpting two poses of Daisy, one sitting and one standing. I thought they were terribly cute, and imagined Suzette would be thrilled with the way they turned out. When I called to see if I could bring them over, Eldon answered the phone.

"Suzette's not here," he said. "She took Tommy to the Urgent Care Center in Bloomington. He had to get stitches in his head."

"Oh no!" I exclaimed. "What happened?"

Eldon chuckled. "He got into a fight. That's Tommy for you. He's nothing but a grown-up kid."

I'd already developed a deep resentment toward Tommy Crawford, but that bit of news made me hate him. I knew his presence in Suzette's life boded nothing but trouble.

"I'll tell her you called," Eldon said.

The following day, I waited all morning for Suzette to return my call. At noon, when I still hadn't heard from her, I decided to call her. Eldon answered the phone again.

"Suzette's still in bed," he told me. "Let me see if she's awake." A few moments later, he said, "She's up now. I'll hand the phone to her. Here she is."

"Lanie, is that you?" a groggy Suzette mumbled. "God, I'm so tired. I'm so tired I can't think straight."

Then she regaled me with the graphic details of her trip to the Urgent Care Center: the amount of blood that had gushed from Tommy's head wound, how he'd used up an entire roll of paper towels trying to stop the flow. "Eldon had to shampoo the upholstery in my car this morning," she said, "because there was blood everywhere."

She told me she and Tommy had been forced to wait an hour at the Urgent Care Center. Tommy had gotten mad and walked out, and she'd had to chase him down and coax him back into the building. The doctor had been rude, and Tommy swore at him and made a big scene. Suzette had been afraid he would be denied treatment.

When I finally managed to get a word in, I asked if she'd like to see my sculptures of Daisy. "Not today, honey," she said. "I'm too worn out."

The following week when I called to see if I could bring my sculptures over, Suzette cut me off quickly. "Tommy's here," she said. "I'm getting ready to take him to the store."

The next time I called, she wasn't home, and Eldon told me she'd taken Tommy to Columbus to apply for a job.

The third time I asked if I could come over, she said, "No, honey, I promised Tommy I'd drive him to his friend's house this evening."

Anger boiled inside me. "Can't your nephew drive himself anywhere?"

Suzette responded calmly to my agitation, speaking slowly and deliberately as if to a clueless child. "No, Lanie, he can't drive himself anywhere. He doesn't have a driver's license."

"Well, don't you think it's about time he got one?"

"He can't. His license has been suspended for life."

Taken aback by this piece of information, I was speechless for a moment. Then Suzette said, "Haven't you figured it out, Lanie? Tommy's an alcoholic."

Suddenly, the puzzle pieces fell into place, and the completed picture made sense to me: Tommy's prison term, his tremors, his fighting, his inability to drive himself anywhere. Of course. Tommy Crawford was a drunk.

"Why on earth do you want someone like this in your life?" I asked, bitterness in my voice. "You know he's not good for you."

"Lanie, you and I have no right to judge Tommy." Suzette spoke in a patronizing tone, as if trying to teach her naïve young friend an important life lesson. "We've all got problems. Just because Tommy has a drinking problem doesn't mean he isn't a worthwhile person. God loves Tommy Crawford just as much as he loves you and me."

I knew if I argued with her, I'd be fighting a losing battle. "Do you ever want to see the sculptures I did of Daisy?" I asked.

"Of course," Suzette said. "Sometime." Her voice softened. "I haven't forgotten about you, Lanie. We'll get together soon."

"What breed do you want me to sculpt next?"

"Oh, I don't know. Maybe a golden retriever or something like that. You figure it out, Lanie."

When I hung up the phone, I was so frustrated with Suzette that I swore to myself I wasn't going to sculpt another damn thing for her. I knew full well she was too distracted to follow through with molding the Chihuahua figurines, or any other breed I might sculpt.

I hadn't told her that I'd already started sculpting a bulldog. I looked at the half-finished piece sitting on my table, and on an angry impulse, I smashed it with my fist. Then I hurled the lump of clay into my trash can, muttering, "I'm done with Suzette and her crazy business."

But when I looked at my two Chihuahua sculptures, I didn't have the heart to ruin them. If Suzette didn't want them, I'd keep them for myself.

I heard from Suzette a week later, on a Saturday afternoon. "Lanie," she whimpered, "can you come over this evening? I need someone to keep me company."

I wanted to be sarcastic and say, "What about your precious Tommy?" But I sensed she was in genuine distress, and I couldn't bring myself to be unkind.

That evening, as we sat in her studio painting nativity figurines, I could tell she was having difficulty staying focused. Finally, she put down her brush and said, "I'm just not going to get this done, Lanie. Not this year."

"What's going on?" I asked.

"I'm worried sick," she said. "Tommy's out drinking tonight, and I know he's going to get plastered. Every time he goes out with his friend Bob, he ends up in trouble one way or the other. I won't be able to relax until I know he got home safely."

"Where does Tommy live?"

"Right now, he's staying with his mom and Oscar. I told his mom to call me when he gets home."

Once again, I allowed myself to ask the obvious question. "Why do you put up with him, Suzette? He's sucking the life out of you. I'm not worried about him. I'm worried about what he's doing to you."

She gazed at me, a weary expression on her face. "You just don't understand, do you Lanie?"

"No," I said. "I don't understand at all."

"Then let me tell you why I can't turn Tommy away." She paused for a long moment, a faraway look in her eyes. "He and I are kindred spirits. Closer than that, actually. We're soul mates. We've always been that way, even when we were kids. We're so close that we read each other's thoughts. I've never had this with anyone else, Lanie. It's a beautiful thing.

"Tommy and I both know what it's like to live with addictions. He has his alcohol, I have my junk food. Tommy knows his alcohol is going to kill him. We're honest with each other, we talk about that. And I know my diabetes is killing me. Everybody hounds me about sticking to my diet, but I can't, and I know I never will. Just like Tommy is never going to lay off the booze. We understand that about each other.

"We understand each other in every way, Lanie. Sometimes we talk about his childhood, being abused by that son-of-a-bitch Oscar. I've told him about what Oscar and my other brothers did to me. Tommy's the only one who knows what it was really like."

She sighed deeply, her tired body sagging. "Lanie, I know Tommy's life is out of control. You don't have to tell me that. The alcohol is going to kill him. But I hope it's later rather than sooner. I'm not ready to lose him yet."

CHAPTER 25

Suzette didn't invite me to Thanksgiving dinner that year. I didn't expect her to, as I figured her holiday would be all about Tommy. So I ended up spending the day with Nana, my mother, and our elderly relatives.

My mother's eyes lit up when she saw me, and she hugged me like she didn't want to let me go. "I miss you, honey," she whispered in my ear. And I realized that, other than exchanging a few words with her at her teller window, I'd spoken to her less than a dozen times the past year.

"It's good to have you with us, Elaine," Nana said. I sensed she no longer took my presence for granted.

That night, I lay in bed taking stock of what I'd been through during the past year: the hair-raising weeks with Jesse Jordan, the hope and the heart-break with Aaron Matthews, and the Tommy-related drama in Suzette's life. I concluded that the year had been the most tumultuous one of my life.

"I'm sick and tired of all this crap," I muttered aloud. "God, I sure hope you have something better in store for me next year."

Then I thought about my soft-spoken, non-demanding, utterly predictable mother, the loving mother I had neglected for years in my efforts to avoid Nana. I decided spending time with her might be good for me.

One of my mother's favorite projects was coordinating the children's Christmas pageant at St. Augustine's. Even though I hadn't been to church in more than a year, I decided to ask her if she could use my help with the program.

My offer delighted her. "Oh yes, honey," she said. "I have lots of costumes to sew. Want to help with that?"

One of my most vivid childhood memories is of my quiet little mother seated at her whirring sewing machine, a half-smile on her thin face, her slender fingers expertly guiding the fabric under the pressure foot. Her fine, straight hair would fall forward like a curtain on each side of her face, and she'd occasionally lift a hand to tuck it behind her ears.

"Everyone needs some activity to settle their nerves," she'd say. "Sewing does it for me."

Each summer, she'd enter a project in the county 4-H fair: a dress, a baby quilt, a pair of rag dolls. More often than not, she'd earn a blue or purple ribbon. I was glad she had something of her own, something outside the realm of Nana's interest and influence.

After I'd moved out of the house, she'd turned my old bedroom into a sewing room, setting up her Singer sewing machine, an ironing board, and a long table for cutting out patterns. The drawers of my old dresser now held scraps of fabric, packets of trim, and spools of thread.

That December, instead of spending Saturday afternoons in Suzette's messy studio, I spent long weekend hours in my mother's immaculate sewing room, cutting out pageant costumes from bolts of cloth while she efficiently fed the pieces through her sewing machine.

"Did Jesse Jordan finally leave you alone?" she asked one afternoon as she pressed the seams of a shepherd's cloak.

"Yes," I replied. "He hasn't bothered me since March or April."

"Good," she said. "I was afraid for you. No mother wants to see her daughter go through something like that."

My mother rarely mustered the confidence to engage in

such intimate conversations with me, as the minute I'd been born, Nana had snatched me out of the arms of her daughter and had taken over my upbringing. I wondered what other challenges my mother had silently and helplessly watched me go through, what other trials of mine had pained her maternal heart.

Then I told her about Aaron. "I really cared about that man, Mom. I thought we'd be perfect together."

She looked up from hand-stitching gold trim around an angel's wing. "I know how you feel, honey. It seems like the best ones get taken from us. It's hard to get over something like that."

I knew she was talking about my father, and I wondered if I should tell her about my other-worldly encounter with him in Suzette's meditation room. I decided not to. I was pretty sure she'd find the news disturbing, and I didn't want to upset her quiet little world.

But I did tell her about sculpting for Suzette, and that piqued her interest. "I'd like to see something you've done," she said.

So the next time I came to the house, I brought the Chihuahua sculptures with me. "Suzette wanted us to do a line of dog breeds," I explained. "But she has a lot of problems right now, and I think she's lost interest."

My mother held one of the Chihuahuas in the palm of her hand, petting its tiny back with a delicate finger. "These are precious, honey," she said. "You should keep doing this. Just because someone else loses interest doesn't mean that you should stop doing something you enjoy."

I sat there savoring her rare offering of motherly wisdom, perhaps the most profound piece of advice she'd ever given me. "You know what?" I said. "I think you're right."

She carefully placed the figurine back in the box I'd packed it in, lovingly tucking the tissue paper around it. "Do you know Margaret Brown?"

I shook my head.

"Your grandmother knows her from the Art Guild. She has a ceramics studio and gallery on Franklin Street in Nashville. She could fire these for you. She could fire anything you do. You should ask her."

"I will," I promised.

I truly meant to leave Suzette alone for awhile. But one mid-December evening, as my mother and I sat at Nana's dining room table addressing Christmas cards, I thought about my friends in Helmsburg. I didn't have the heart to pass them up, and I selected a card I thought Suzette would particularly enjoy.

Three days later, she called to thank me for the card. "I miss you, Lanie," she said, her voice wistful. "I wanted to wish you a Merry Christmas. But I can't seem to get myself together to send out cards this year. It's been so crazy around here."

"What's going on?" I asked.

The next instant, I regretted my question, as Suzette immediately launched into the latest breaking news in the life of her nephew. "We're moving Tommy in here this weekend. Would you believe that son-of-a-bitch Oscar threw him out of the house?"

She didn't mention Oscar's reason for doing such a thing, but it didn't take much imagination on my part to figure out why. Son-of-a-bitch or not, I couldn't blame Oscar for not wanting his forty-five-year-old alcoholic stepson under his roof.

"I couldn't see leaving Tommy homeless at Christmastime," she said.

"Suzette," I cautioned. "You know how I feel about this. I'm afraid for you."

"I know, I know," she sighed. "Everybody's against me on this."

"What's Eldon saying?"

"Well, he's not keen on the idea. But I told him I'd put Tommy in the basement. That way, he'll be out of our hair. I moved my table out of the meditation room and set up a cot for him in there."

"Oh no!" I protested. "You're giving up your meditation room? How could you do that? That room is important to you, Suzette. It's your space, not his."

"Well, Lanie," she huffed, "whether we like it or not, things change. I can be sitting here in my chair minding my own goddamn business, and something happens outside my window that completely changes my life. I figure I might as well go along with it. It's going to happen anyway."

CHAPTER 26

After the flurry of holiday activity, January brought me solitude, more peace and quiet than I actually needed. Brown County was blanketed with one snowstorm after another, and I barely got my driveway cleared for my clients before another storm hit.

I was so tired that I slept ten hours at night and took naps during the day. I asked myself whether I was depressed, but I didn't think so. It was more like I was hibernating, replenishing my depleted reserves, storing up energy for what was to come.

Between snowstorms, I managed to drive to Joann Fabrics in Columbus, where I bought several yards of red velvet fabric. On my way home, I stopped at Nana's house and asked my mother to hem the cloth.

"What's this for?" she asked as she fed the fabric through her sewing machine.

"My meditation table," I replied.

She looked perplexed. "Oh?"

Then I told her about meditating with Suzette, and why that was no longer possible. "You said I shouldn't stop doing something I enjoy just because someone else lost interest. Meditating is good for me, and I'm going to keep doing it."

My mother looked enormously pleased to learn that I'd valued her bit of advice. "Good for you, honey," she said.

I took the red velvet fabric home and draped it over an old coffee table that I'd lugged up the stairs and set up in the corner of my bedroom. Then, with great precision, I placed a candle in the center of it. The table seemed a little too empty, but it occurred to me that, over time, I might decorate it with other items of importance to me.

The other thing I accomplished that snowy January was to make it down to Margaret Brown's gallery and studio. This was the first time I'd met the diminutive sixty-year-old artist, and as I looked around at the magnificent pieces in her gallery, the silly little figures I sculpted for Suzette seemed ridiculous. Suddenly, I didn't feel good enough to ask a favor on my own merit, and as much as I hated to play the card, I resorted to identifying myself as Arlene Greene's granddaughter. Margaret readily agreed to allow space in her kiln for any projects I wanted to fire.

After looking over my Chihuahua figurines, she said, "Hmm. You certainly have an aptitude for sculpting. Have you ever taken ceramics classes?"

"Not since high school," I told her.

"I'm thinking about starting a class here in the studio. Soon, maybe next month. I only have room for a few students at a time. Would you be interested?"

"Absolutely," I said.

"Good," she said. "I'll call you when I'm ready to start."

At least you have one thing to look forward to, I told myself on the drive home. I pulled my car into the garage, then trudged down to the end of my long drive and grabbed a handful of mail out of my mailbox. When I got inside, I flung the mail on the kitchen table and climbed the stairs to my bedroom for another winter nap.

In the early evening, I got up and made myself a bowl of soup, then sat down at the table to go through my mail.

I glanced at a utility bill, several items of junk mail, and a late Christmas card from a friend. Then I picked up a small envelope on which my name and address were printed in awkwardly formed letters.

What the heck is this? I wondered. I opened the envelope and pulled out a single sheet of lined paper that had been torn from a small tablet. The contents stunned me.

> *"When you walked into the room, you lit up my world. You were the most beautiful woman I had ever seen. This poor man can't stop thinking about you."*

The brief letter, printed in the same awkward hand as on the envelope, was full of spelling errors. I got the distinct impression that the sender didn't often communicate through the written word. There was no signature. I picked up the envelope again and saw that there was no return address. Nothing at all to identify the man who'd sent it.

I stared at the paper, wide-eyed. The element of mystery stimulated me, woke me up from my January stupor. My mind reeled with possibilities.

Was it Jesse Jordan trying to wiggle his way back into my life? No. Jesse was certainly more literate than to produce this crudely scrawled note. And he was too focused on his own image to dwell on the charms of a woman.

Was it Aaron? For a moment, I hoped it was, but the letter couldn't possibly have been written by a college graduate. And Aaron had never used such flowery language with me.

Then I considered the possibility that my secret admirer might be one of my massage clients. I shuddered as I thought about the problems that would pose for me. But as I looked back over the past few months, I realized that I hadn't taken on a new male client in quite some time, and none of my longstanding clients showed the slightest sign of romantic interest in me.

Where had I recently walked into a room where some man saw me for the first time? I searched my mind for places I'd gone in the past month. I'd been out shopping for groceries and Christmas gifts, but I didn't get the sense that the man had seen me in a crowded store. I'd been at Nana's house a number of times, but had encountered no men there other than my great-uncles Harvey and Melvin.

I'd also been to church two or three times in the past month. I mentally ran through the list of men at St. Augustine's. They'd all known me for years, so none of them could have experienced the letter writer's awe associated with a first-time meeting.

All my rational speculation took me to a dead end, leaving me with nothing but mystery. Smiling to myself, I laid the letter on top of my dresser. I'd have to wait for the answer to reveal itself.

Three days later, I received a second letter in the same crude hand, printed on a sheet of paper that appeared to be torn from the same small tablet.

> *"I smile every time I think about you. I wish you could know how I feel about you. I know I can make you the happiest woman in the world, if you will only give me the chance."*

As I read the note, excitement and fear coursed through my body simultaneously. I could think of only one person who would appreciate such drama. I picked up the phone and called Suzette. She answered in a weary voice.

"You won't believe what's happening to me," I said. "Some secret admirer is sending me letters. Listen to this." Then I read the contents of the notes to her.

"Oh, Lanie!" she exclaimed, suddenly energized. "This is so romantic! Do you have any idea who it is?"

"Not at all," I said. "There's no signature and no return address. I've wracked my brain for days, trying to figure out who could've sent them, and I've come up with nothing."

"Why don't you bring the letters over here and let me see them?" she suggested. "Maybe we can figure it out together."

"Okay," I said. "When do you want me to come?"

"Well, we can't do it any day this week. I have to take Tommy to work."

"He's working now?"

"Oh yes, he got a job at a factory in Columbus last week. I have to drive him there every morning, and then pick him up in the evening."

"Wow," I said. "That's a lot on you."

"I know," she said. "But I'm so proud of him. I just hope this job will be the incentive for him to turn his life around. I'd do anything to help him get on the right track."

She babbled on about Tommy for awhile before bringing the conversation back to me and my secret admirer. "Can you come Sunday afternoon? Tommy will be at his friend's house, and Eldon will probably be sleeping. We can have the place to ourselves."

Four days later, on Saturday, I received the third letter from my mystery man.

> *"I hope these letters aren't making you nervous. I can't help it, I have to write them. Please don't be afraid. I would never hurt someone I love. You have no idea what you mean to me. I know in my heart we are meant to be together. Someday, you will feel the same way I do."*

At that moment, I felt no emotion but fear. *Oh my God,* I thought. *Do I need to take this to the police?* I placed the letter on my dresser with the other two, ready for Suzette's perusal.

When Suzette greeted me at the door the next day, I was aghast at how much weight she'd lost. Her shabby blouse and slacks hung loosely on her large frame. Dark smudges underlined her tired eyes.

"Suzette, you're getting so thin!" I exclaimed. "Have you been ill?"

She waved her hand dismissively. "My doctor's been on me for years to lose weight. He should be happy now."

When I stepped into the living room, I saw that the clutter in the Perrys' home had risen to new proportions. A half-empty plate of food sat on the coffee table, along with three beer cans.

"Excuse this mess," Suzette said, sweeping her hand around the room. "That damn Tommy. I tell him over and over that if he's going to drink, he has to do it in the basement. But he comes up after Eldon and I have gone to bed and sits here drinking and watching TV."

She moved some newspapers off the sofa and threw Daisy's blanket on the floor, making room for me to sit down. I pulled the letters out of my bag and handed them to her.

She sat down next to me and took each of the letters out of their envelopes in turn. As she read them, her face darkened. Then she handed them back to me.

"That stupid jerk!" she exclaimed. "I had a sneaking suspicion it was him. I had to see the handwriting to make sure."

"Who?" I asked.

"Tommy. Your secret admirer is Tommy."

"You're kidding me!"

She shook her head. "Nope. He's had a thing for you ever since he saw you that one time. When was it?"

"Last October," I said.

"He keeps asking when you're coming over again. Every time he talks about you, he gets nervous and starts shaking. He's fallen hard for you, Lanie."

I stared at her, incredulous.

"I keep telling him that a girl like you wouldn't want anything to do with a guy like him. But he won't believe me. He thinks you were leading him on that day you met him. Remember when you asked him about his art? I told him you were just being polite, but he's convinced you had feelings for him.

"That's why I can't have you coming over here when he's around. You'll get him all stirred up. He might be an idiot, but I care about him, and I don't want him to get hurt."

Suddenly, I couldn't stand to hold the revolting letters any longer, and I threw them on the coffee table. "That's just gross!" I blurted out.

Suzette reached out and swept the letters together with her big hands, then tapped them on the table to line up the edges. "Lanie, you don't have to be nasty about it. He doesn't mean you any harm. I'll make him stop. If he writes you another letter, let me know, and I'll slap him silly."

I drove home feeling decidedly depressed, and when I got there, I climbed the stairs and crawled into bed for yet another January nap.

CHAPTER 27

"Has Tommy written you any more letters?" Suzette asked when she phoned me two weeks later.

"No," I said, "he hasn't."

"Good," she said. "I didn't think he would, but I wanted to make sure. We had a big showdown over it. I told him you came over here with the letters, all upset."

I smiled, knowing that Suzette had embellished the facts of the story in order to make her point with Tommy.

"I told him he needed to leave you alone," she continued. "He blew up and said I had no right to tell him what to do. I just pointed to the door and told him if he didn't like my rules, he could leave. Then he simmered down. He's cool right now."

I shuddered, imagining the hair-raising scene between the two of them. "Are you still driving Tommy to work every day?" I asked.

"Well, no, not now. He lost his job in Columbus a couple of weeks ago. He got pissed off at a coworker and took a swing at him. I sat him down and said, 'Tommy, I love you, but you're driving me crazy. You're forty-five years old. You need to start acting like an adult. You've got to learn to get along with people. If somebody's getting on your nerves, you need to ignore them. Just tune them out. You can't be swinging at everyone who makes you mad. No boss is going to put up with that kind of bullshit.'"

"Good for you," I said.

She sighed. "I don't know whether it sunk in. His buddy got him a job where he works in Indianapolis. They ride together, so I'm off the hook as far as transportation goes. Tommy's doing pretty well so far, except that he hates getting up early. Every morning, I have a fight on my hands when I try to get him out of bed. Especially if he's had a lot to drink the night before."

"You have to get him up?" I asked, incredulous.

"It doesn't hurt me to do that much for him," she said. "At least I can go back to bed and get some more sleep after he and Eldon are both out of the house."

"Suzette, are you taking care of yourself?" I scolded. "Are you watching your diet and taking your medication? I'm afraid you'll get so wrapped up in Tommy that you'll let your own health go down the tubes."

She chuckled. "You know me, Lanie. I never stick to my diet. But I take my insulin shots when my sugar gets too high. I won't forget to do that. I promise."

I was surprised when Suzette called me again, just three days later. "Lanie," she whimpered, "I need somebody to talk to."

"What's going on?" I asked.

"Tommy invited a bunch of his friends to a party at our house last night. Lanie, they acted like a bunch of wild animals. You should see my house now. It's completely trashed, and none of those sons-of-bitches are here today to help me clean up the mess. You remember that cute little set of mugs Eldon got me for my birthday last year? The ones with the hearts on them? Well, two of them got broken. Nobody would admit to doing it. And some dude puked all over the couch. The house stinks like hell."

"Oh my God, Suzette," I exclaimed. "That's awful!"

"That isn't even half of it," she said. "Tommy and some others were out on the new deck Eldon built, and they started horsing around. Somebody kicked three spindles out of the railing. Tommy always gets mean after he has five or six beers. Some guy was mouthing off at him, and he picked up my lawn chair and clobbered him. He broke the damn chair.

"Eldon bought me that chair just last summer, and I was looking forward to using it when the weather gets warm again. It was so comfortable.

"You know, Lanie, everybody talks about how beautiful California is, but the only part of California I ever knew was slums and rundown apartment buildings. When Eldon and I moved here, I was so grateful to be surrounded by nature again. Then he built that deck, and I loved stretching out on my new chair, just staring out into the woods and listening to the birds and the rippling of the creek. Now my chair's broken, and I can't do that anymore."

"I'm so sorry, Suzette," I said.

She was so wrapped up in her story that she didn't seem to hear my interjection. "Anyway, that dude picked Tommy up and threw him off the deck. I was scared to death somebody was going to get hurt. I went out there and yelled at them to knock it off. The back yard was all muddy because of the snow melting. When Tommy got up, he was covered with mud, head to toe." She laughed. "You should've seen him, Lanie. It was hilarious."

Then she resumed her complaining tone. "I made Tommy go to the bathroom to clean up. Of course, he tracked mud all through the house. I was just too tired to do anything about it, and I decided to go to my bedroom and lie down. And guess what I found when I opened the bedroom door."

"I don't think I even want to know," I said.

"Some guy and girl were going at it, right on my bed. Can you believe anybody having the nerve to do something like that? I told them to get the hell out of there."

"Unbelievable," I murmured.

"Lanie," she sighed, "I was so upset after that party that I didn't sleep a wink last night. I'm exhausted. I don't know how I'm going to get this place cleaned up."

I wondered whether she was trying to elicit an offer from me to come over and help her. But there was no way I was going to join her in cleaning up Tommy Crawford's mess. "Why did you let this go on?" I asked. "It's your house. You didn't have to let those low-lifes come over."

"I didn't think it would get this out of hand." Her voice sounded defensive. "I just wanted people to have a good time."

"What did Eldon say about what happened?"

"Nothing yet," she muttered. "And he'd better not say anything. If he doesn't want to pay attention to me, he can't blame me for having a social life. At least Tommy and his friends talk to me. My God, Lanie, I could go freaking nuts sitting here night after night with my boob of a husband."

Suzette's frazzled post-party call marked the beginning of a pattern, calls I came to dread. They always started out with her complaining bitterly about the outrageous behavior of Tommy and his friends. Then she'd wind around to her inevitable conclusion, her justification for keeping those loathsome individuals in her life.

I gave up confronting her, as doing so was pointless. Sometimes, I asked myself why I wasted my time listening to her nonsense. Then I'd remember the times she'd been there for me, the times she came through when my world seemed like it was falling apart. Now I sensed that she was the one in trouble, plunging deeper and deeper into something from which she couldn't extricate herself. I felt compelled to keep a watchful eye on her.

In March, Suzette called me more distraught than usual. "This morning when I tried to get Tommy up for work, he swung at me. If I wouldn't have jumped back, he would've hit me hard, right in the stomach. I went upstairs and told Eldon what he'd done. I guess Eldon was fed up. He went tearing down the stairs and told Tommy to get out of the house. He told him if he wasn't gone in fifteen minutes, he was going to call the cops."

I had a hard time imagining Suzette's goofy little husband getting that fired up, and I put my hand over the receiver so she couldn't hear me laughing.

"It got really ugly, Lanie," she whimpered. "Tommy said he was sick and tired of us telling him what to do. He said we were too screwed up ourselves to try to run anybody else's life. He called us names that would make your hair curl. It hurts my heart every time I think about it. He said he'd leave when he got good and ready. So Eldon went out to the garage and got a two-by-four and acted like he was going to beat Tommy with it. I guess that scared him enough to make him leave. I don't know where he went. He'll probably end up staying with one of his friends."

She began to sob. "I know he didn't mean it, Lanie. I know Tommy loves me. He's a sick man. It was just his addiction talking. Deep down, Tommy has a beautiful soul. Not everybody knows that, but I do. I just wish I could've done something more to help him. I feel like I failed him."

"Suzette," I said. "I know you don't want to hear this, but I'm glad Tommy's gone. I'm practically doing cartwheels over this. I was so afraid he'd take you down with him.

Maybe now you can get back on track with your own life."

"You're right, Lanie," she sniffled. "Maybe I can get back to working on my business again. But right now, I'm too tired to do anything."

"Guess what," I said. "Next week, I'm going to start sculpting classes at Margaret Brown's studio in Nashville. That should help me improve my work. Who knows what I can do for your business after that?"

"You're moving on to bigger and better things," Suzette said, her voice wistful. "I'm going to lose you, too, Lanie."

I wanted to tell her that it was her own damn fault, that she'd pushed me away for the sake of her good-for-nothing nephew. But I knew that would be unkind.

"You'll never lose me," I promised her.

That evening, I sat at my velvet-shrouded meditation table, staring at the candle flame, missing Suzette's labored breathing, her wise presence. *How did everything change so abruptly?* I asked myself. *Why has Suzette's life suddenly plunged into such turmoil?*

Then it occurred to me that, for her, nothing had changed. She was still living out the frenetic misadventures of her hair-raising California life, only this chapter was taking place in Helmsburg, Indiana. She was following Tommy Crawford down a path of destruction, just like she'd done with her California husbands.

"Suzette, why do you need this mess?" I whispered. "How is it that you know how to guide me, yet your own life is out of control?"

I knew she'd never be able to respond to such questions. She'd buried the answers, hiding them from herself.

CHAPTER 28

That spring, I got so caught up with my lessons at Margaret Brown's studio that my concerns about Suzette and her chaotic life drifted into the back of my mind.

Like Suzette, my new mentor was blunt-speaking. I had to learn to welcome her criticism of my work and not take it to heart. Margaret's short, spiky, gray hair reflected her lack of concern for conventional appearances, and every time I saw the wiry little woman, she was wearing jeans and an oversized, clay-stained denim shirt.

The lessons took me far beyond the dinky little figurines I'd made for Suzette's business. Margaret first introduced me to portrait sculpting, teaching me the variations of the human head. Then I moved on to life-size sculptures, gaining an understanding of the balance, proportion, and anatomy of the human figure. I learned to start a project by making an armature, and then adding mass and form with the clay. My massage work had familiarized me with the body, and I was delighted to discover that this experience became an asset in my sculpting.

In addition to being a sculptor, Margaret was also a potter. She taught me wheel-throwing, and how to add color and ornamentation through the firing process.

I was so enthralled with my work that I could hardly tear myself away from the studio. All thoughts about finding a boyfriend left my mind. Working with clay had become the new love of my life, a love that wouldn't threaten me, deceive me, or abandon me. My affair with sculpting was safe and satisfying, completely under my control.

My mother became my biggest fan, and she took to stopping by the studio to see the latest project I was working on. Then Nana heard Margaret talking about my work in town. One day, she came by to see what I was doing.

She strutted around my workspace, looking down her nose through her red-framed bifocals, picking up and examining my smooth glazed pots, running her fingers over the cold clay of a half-finished sculpture.

"My goodness, Elaine," she finally said. "I didn't know you had this in you. You never cease to amaze me."

"Thank you, Nana," I said. Then I looked away to hide my smile. I knew I'd provided her with another credential to add to her illustrious social resume. Having a sculptor for a granddaughter would be something else she could brag about to her snooty friends.

Margaret also instructed me in the ancient art of mold-making: building a proper seam wall, applying a splash coat, building up each side of the mother mold, releasing the mold, preparing the print, and doing a final casting of the sculpture. One day, I told myself that my newly acquired ability to make molds rendered me capable of continuing my work independently of Suzette. When I heard my own smug thought, I felt ashamed, so when I got home, I picked up the phone and called my old friend.

"I'm just wondering how you are," I told her. "I haven't heard from you in ages."

"Oh, I'm fine, honey," Suzette said glibly. "I have lots to tell you, but I can't talk long right now. I'm getting ready to go out. Tommy and I are going to Frankie's Pub in Morgantown."

My heart sank. "So Tommy's back in your life?"

She was silent for a moment, and when she spoke again, her voice sounded defensive. "Well, Tommy doesn't live here anymore, if that's what you want to know. Eldon won't allow it. But a couple of weeks after he moved out, he came back around and said he was sorry for acting like a jerk. So we started talking and hanging out again."

I was certain that Tommy had some ulterior motive for reconnecting with Suzette. He probably needed a ride or wanted to borrow money he'd never pay back.

"How can you trust him?" I asked. "After everything he's done to you?"

Suzette sighed with exasperation. "Lanie, you don't understand. I know it's not going to be easy having Tommy in my life. He's going to challenge me. He's even going to lie to me sometimes. I know that. I'm not stupid. But I need to keep an eye on him. I have to. Deep down, I know that's the right thing to do. Tommy and I have a relationship that goes way back."

"I know, I know," I said, irritated by her foolish sentiment. "You told me you used to take care of him when you were children."

"I mean before that," she said. "Some other lifetime. Probably many lifetimes. Tommy and I have a cosmic connection that nobody understands. I don't even understand it myself."

I remained silent, knowing the futility of arguing with her fantasy.

"I know you don't believe me, Lanie," she continued. "If you'd ever had an experience like this, you'd know what I'm talking about."

The tone of superiority in her voice made my blood boil. I knew she viewed Tommy and herself as occupying a higher realm than the rest of us ordinary mortals.

"I have such beautiful dreams about him and me

together," she said wistfully. "They're so surreal, and the love we share is so beautiful. They're always in some strange setting I don't recognize. I know it's about the past lives we shared. I know we're soul mates. That's why I need to look out for him, just as much as I need to look out for myself."

I couldn't hide the sarcasm in my response. "So you're going to Frankie's Pub just to babysit him?"

"Well, not entirely. I know that if he starts heading for trouble, I can jump in and steer him in a different direction. But I like to have a good time myself once in a while. There's nothing wrong with that."

"You can't drink, Suzette," I pointed out. "With your health problems and all the medication you're on, you can't start drinking."

"Don't worry. I'll try to stick to my diet Coke."

"You'll try?"

"Well, Lanie, I can't be perfect all the time."

I stood there shaking my head in disbelief, glad she couldn't see me from the other end of the line. *I can't stand to watch this. She's going downhill fast, and there's nothing I can do about it. I need to back off and let her do what she thinks she needs to do.*

As if she heard my thoughts, Suzette said, "I'll be all right, Lanie, I promise. I'll call you tomorrow and tell you all about it."

"Okay," I said. I didn't believe she would, and I hoped she wouldn't.

But the next morning, my phone rang at 7:30, while I was getting ready for my first massage appointment. It was Suzette.

"Lanie, I had such a wonderful time last night!" she chortled.

"I can't believe you're up this early," I said. "I'm barely awake myself."

"Oh, I haven't been to bed yet. I just got in a couple of hours ago, and I've been too excited to sleep."

"So what happened?"

"I met all kinds of people at Frankie's Pub. There were a few people I went to school with in Morgantown. You know that's my hometown, don't you?"

"Yes," I said. "You told me that."

"It was so good talking to them. And I also I met a bunch of new people. I sat in the back booth with my diet Coke, talking to people for hours, one person after another. They started telling me all kinds of things about their lives. You wouldn't believe the messes people get themselves into."

Oh yes I would, I thought.

"I must look like someone people can trust, because they'll tell me anything. Maybe I should've been a counselor."

On and on she babbled, about who told her what problem and what advice she'd given them.

I finally had to cut her off. "Suzette, I need to go. I have a client coming in ten minutes."

"Sorry," she said. "I've got so much more to tell you. I'm going to bed now. I'll call you when I get up."

That evening, she called again. "Have you ever been to the Bean Blossom Dragway?"

"No," I said. "I haven't even heard of it. Where is it?"

"It's on Spearsville Road. Tommy's taking me there tomorrow night. Have you ever watched drag-racing?"

"No, I haven't."

"I just love all the excitement of it. I can't wait to go. I'd invite you to come along, but I don't want Tommy to get all stirred up again. He still asks about you, and I know if he sees you, he'll start acting stupid all over again. We don't want that."

"No, we don't," I said emphatically.

"Oh, Lanie, I had the best time of my life!" Suzette exclaimed when she called to report on her first outing to the drag-strip. She carried on and on about the souped-up cars and their good-looking drivers. "But I couldn't see as much as I wanted to. I had to sit at the bottom of the bleachers. I couldn't climb up to the top because my legs hurt too bad. Tommy went up to the top and sat there all evening. That hurt my feelings. You'd think he'd be considerate enough to stick with me. After all, I was the one who drove him there."

Tommy has never considered you, Suzette, I thought. *He knows nothing about that deep connection you think you have with him. He's only out for what he can get.*

The second time Suzette and Tommy went to the dragway, they took Eldon with them. "I didn't want him to feel left out," Suzette told me. "But, oh my God, Lanie. He sat there like a bump on a log. Didn't talk to a soul, just sat there with a blank look on that stupid face of his. I was so embarrassed. When we got home, I asked him why he acted like that. He said he wasn't interested in drag-racing. Can you imagine that, Lanie? Who wouldn't be interested in drag-racing?"

I'm not interested in it, I thought. But there was no interrupting her anti-Eldon rant.

"It's so exciting. It's a wonderful place to meet people, and it's good, clean fun. I'm not taking Eldon again, that's for sure."

When I hung up the phone, I felt profoundly sorry for Suzette's husband. Good old Eldon, who cleaned up his wife's messes, who ran interference for her when things got tough, who did everything she couldn't manage on her own. I wondered how long he'd put up with her.

CHAPTER 29

That summer, I often regretted having reconnected with Suzette, as every couple of weeks, she called to update me on the social life she shared with her nephew. Each time, she'd complain bitterly about the stupid behavior of the people with whom she was keeping company.

I sometimes found myself on the verge of saying, "Suzette, I don't want to hear this." Then I'd remember all the times she'd treated me with love and compassion, and I knew I couldn't turn my back on her. So I forced myself to sit through her chaotic ramblings, trying to find the humor in her bizarre stories.

I gave up on asking the obvious question: "If they make you so angry, why do you hang out with people like that?" After she'd vent her frustrations, she'd inevitably come around to justifying her choice in friends.

Of course, she always drove wherever she and Tommy went, and en route to their destination, she'd pick up one or more of his shiftless friends, Greg, Mike, or Steve.

"We were at Frankie's Pub for hours last night," she complained to me one day. "I was getting really tired, and I wanted to go home. Tommy and Mike and Steve all got in the car when I told them it was time to leave, but Greg didn't. I told Tommy to go back into the bar and get Greg, but every time he tried, Greg would just cuss at him and flip him off. Tommy was getting madder and madder, and I thought there was going to be a fight.

"Finally, Greg came out. I had the engine running and the headlights on. But instead of getting into the car, that damn Greg just stood there in the headlights, doing stupid poses, turning this way and that way, making goofy faces at me. It pissed me off so bad that I almost stepped on the gas and ran him over. I don't need to put up with bullshit like that."

Another time, her drunken friends got so rowdy on the drive home that she had to pull off the side of the road until they settled down. "Just like a bunch of goddamn kids," she complained. "I told them if they didn't shut up, they could all get out and walk home. Next time that happens, I'm going to throw them all out and leave their sorry asses in the ditch."

When Suzette called me after spending Labor Day weekend with Tommy at the drag-strip, I could tell she was in genuine distress. "I'm so upset, Lanie," she whimpered.

"What's going on?" I asked.

"You wouldn't believe what happened last night. I was just sitting there at the bottom of the bleachers like I usually do, watching the races, having a good time. Tommy was sitting at the top, like he always does. There was some dude there from Trevlac, named Earl. Tommy hates his guts. Both of them had had a little bit to drink. Earl was running his mouth, going on and on. I could hear him from down where I was sitting. Just a bunch of bullshit. People were telling him to shut up.

"Finally, Tommy yelled at him at the top of his lungs, 'Shut the fuck up!' I turned around to see what was happening. There was a woman sitting next to Earl holding a soft drink with ice in it. Earl jumped up and grabbed the drink and dumped it over the top of Tommy's head. Tommy got really pissed and shoved him, and Earl fell off the bleachers. He just lay there on the ground, not moving at all.

"Lanie, I was so scared, I was hyperventilating. I thought, *Oh my God, Tommy killed him!* My chest hurt so bad that I thought I was having a heart attack.

"Somebody called 911. The cops came, and then the ambulance. It turned out that Earl only broke his arm. But Tommy was arrested. I'm sure he's going to be doing some time in jail. And the manager of the racetrack told him he wasn't allowed on the property anymore."

Now do you see Tommy for who he is? I wanted to ask her.

"We had such a good thing going on at the drag-strip, and now it's spoiled," she sniffled. "But I don't think it was entirely Tommy's fault. Earl started it."

She was quiet for a moment, and when she spoke again, her voice sounded plaintive. "I don't know what to do with myself now, Lanie. I feel lost."

I wanted to capitalize on the moment and steer her in a different direction. "Maybe you and I can do something together. Do you have anything you want to work on for your business?"

She sighed. "I haven't touched anything in my studio for months. It's a horrible mess. I need to get down there and clean things up, but I wouldn't even know where to start."

"Want me to come over and help?"

"Maybe. I'll let you know when I'm ready."

After I hung up the phone, I sat at my kitchen table staring out the window, thinking. *What am I getting myself into? I'm looking after Suzette the same way she looks after Tommy. She tries to fix his life, and it drags her down. Then I try to fix her problems, and that drags me down. I need to stop this.*

But I found I couldn't turn off my concern about Suzette. Several weeks after the fiasco at the drag-strip, I asked her if she'd like to have dinner with me at Nashville's Brown Sparrow Café. I wanted to prove a point: that her social life didn't need to be fraught with drama, that she could enjoy herself without being surrounded by people who were acting up and making fools of themselves.

I honestly didn't expect her to accept my invitation, so her enthusiastic response surprised me. "Sure, Lanie, that sounds like fun."

The day before our outing, she called me, irritation in her voice. "Eldon wants to know if he's invited to come with us tomorrow night."

Her question caught me off guard. I hadn't planned on including Eldon. But as I thought about the longsuffering fellow who'd sat at home night after night while his wife ran out with her nephew, I decided he deserved something special. "Of course he's invited," I said.

"I've never been here before," Suzette said as we seated ourselves at the wooden table in the Brown Sparrow Café.

"Me neither," Eldon echoed as he glanced around the small room with its wood paneling and homey curtains. "It's a nice place."

Even though I tried not to, I couldn't help but watch Suzette to monitor how she was doing. I wanted her to feel at home in the wholesome environment.

So I was relieved to see her gazing contentedly at the rustic artwork on the walls of the cafe. "I think some of my crafts would look good in here," she said. "Don't you, Lanie? Maybe they'd be interested in buying something from me. We should ask."

When the waitress came to take our orders, Suzette scanned the menu and said, "I'm going all out here. Bring me a bacon cheeseburger. And a large order of onion rings. And a diet Coke." She paused, and then grinned mischievously. "Oh, what the hell. I'll take a chocolate milkshake, too."

She looked at me and wagged a finger. "Lanie, don't you dare lecture me about sticking to my diet."

One of the special features of the Brown Sparrow Café was their live country music. When the small band began playing, Suzette closed her eyes and swayed in her seat, keeping time with the rhythm by tapping her fingers on the table.

"This is a great little place," she said when she opened her eyes again. "I love this band. That guitar player's really cute, isn't he, Lanie? You should go up and talk to him before we leave."

Midway through our meal, one of Nana's Historical Society friends, Thelma Thompson, stopped by our table. "I heard you've been taking lessons from Margaret Brown," she said, patting me on the shoulder. "Your grandmother told me you've been doing some terrific work. I'll have to stop by and see it sometime."

"Thank you," I said. "That would be nice." Then I gestured toward my companions. "These are my friends, Eldon and Suzette Perry. Suzette is the one who got me started in sculpting. I've done some things for her craft business."

Thelma turned her gaze to my frumpy, frizzy-haired friend, and I hoped Suzette didn't see the flicker of disdain in the well-dressed woman's eyes. "Really? What kind of work do you do?"

Beaming, Suzette launched into a description of the craft items she'd created over the years. As she talked proudly about her business, I thought, *Maybe this will motivate her to get back on track with her work.*

Another of Nana's friends, Marjorie Hilton, walked up and greeted me, and then engaged Thelma in a conversation about Historical Society business. While they talked, Suzette nudged me and pointed covertly at Eldon. He'd finished eating and was staring into space, his eyes vacant, a stupid grin on his face.

"See how he is?" Suzette whispered, looking utterly pained.

She and I talked with Thelma and Marjorie a few more minutes, chatting about Margaret Brown's studio, the Brown County Art Gallery, and the latest show at the Brown County Playhouse. I thought Suzette was enjoying the conversation, but after the two women walked away, she looked downcast.

"I was right," she said.

"About what?" I asked.

"I told you that you'd be moving on to bigger and better things. Now you're doing high-class work, hanging out with high-class people. Pretty soon, you won't be giving me the time of day."

"Suzette, that's just crazy!" I scolded. "I keep telling you that any time you're ready to work on your business again, I'll do more sculpting for you. I mean that, I really do. I'm just waiting for the word from you."

She laid her graceful, man-sized hand over mine. "You're so sweet to me, Lanie. I'll let you know when I'm ready."

Behind her impish smile, I could see the dark shadow of her pain.

CHAPTER 30

After our evening at the Brown Sparrow Café, I lost sight of Suzette for awhile. I told myself I'd given everything I could to our friendship. She hadn't taken me up on the multiple offers I'd made to help with her business. There was nothing more I could do to motivate her to get back to work.

I figured she was wearing herself out, running to the jail on the south side of Nashville three times a week to see her beloved Tommy. As much as she could, she'd share the experience of incarceration with him.

She hadn't told me the length of Tommy's jail term. As the weeks passed, I had no idea whether he was still locked up, or whether Suzette was back to driving him to the bars and the homes of his sleazy friends.

At one o'clock on a Saturday morning in mid-November, my telephone rang. When I picked it up, I heard sobbing on the other end of line. Then Suzette's voice whispered, "Lanie, Tommy's dead."

My groggy brain couldn't comprehend what she was saying. "What?"

"Tommy's dead," she repeated.

"Oh my God, Suzette! What happened?"

She lapsed into anguished sobbing, and then the line went dead.

Shaken by the startling call, I lay awake the rest of the night, trying to wrap my mind around the terrible news. *Poor Suzette! How is she going to get through this? What do I need to do? Should I drive over to Helmsburg to be with her?*

At 6:00 AM, I finally got up and called the Perry's home, and Suzette's weary-sounding husband answered the phone.

"Eldon," I said, "Suzette called me about Tommy. What happened?"

"He was hit by a train," Eldon replied. "He was walking home from his friend's house around midnight, not that far from here. Dead drunk, as usual. He was climbing over the tracks that run along State Road 45. He must've fallen down and passed out on the tracks, and a train ran over him."

"Oh, that's terrible!" I exclaimed. "How's Suzette doing? Should I come over and stay with her for awhile?"

"It won't do any good. She was so shook up that I had to give her one of her nerve pills. She's sleeping now. Anyway, she won't talk to anybody. She just cries and cries."

"How are you doing?"

"I'm okay," he sighed. "Somebody around here has got to be okay."

The following week, I called Eldon daily to check on Suzette. Each time, he reported that she wasn't ready to talk to anyone. On the third day, he told me about the plans for Tommy's service at the Bowen-Marshall Funeral Home in Nashville.

"I'll be there," I promised him.

I arrived at the funeral home thirty minutes before the service was scheduled to start, hoping to spend some time with Suzette. When I walked into the room where the service was to be held, I saw that the efforts to memorialize Tommy's life had been minimal. Two small floral arrangements stood beside a closed casket, and only a handful of people milled around the room. Off to one side, I saw a table with a small display of pictures, which I assumed were of Tommy and his loved ones.

Suzette was standing by the casket, leaning heavily on Eldon's arm. I watched as he led her to a chair. She moved like an old woman, as if she'd aged twenty years since I'd last seen her. Her eyes looked haunted. She was wearing an ill-fitting black dress that hung limply on her frame, and her ugly footwear looked like little more than bedroom slippers. I imagined her feet were hurting her terribly.

I walked over and sat down beside her, sliding my arm around her shoulders. "I want you to know I'm here for you, Suzette," I murmured.

Without turning to look at me, she whispered, "Thank you, Lanie."

She continued to sit immobilized, staring vacantly into space. Then she lifted a tired hand and pointed to a young man standing beside the casket. "That's Tommy's son."

Suzette had never mentioned the fact that Tommy was a father. His son, who appeared to be in his early twenties, looked a great deal like him, tall and lanky. His thin face was contorted with pain, his tortured blue eyes brimming with tears. I knew he was grieving for the father who'd never been there for him.

I wanted to walk up to him, to put a hand on his shoulder and say, *Please don't follow the example your father gave you. You can do better than that. You must! Don't throw away your life like he did.*

"I'm going to look at the pictures," I whispered to Suzette. She nodded mutely.

I stood in front of the display of photos that spanned Tommy's lifetime: the laughing face of a chubby baby, the sad, questioning eyes of a blonde-haired schoolboy, the smirk on the face of the young man who'd learned to cover his insecurity with a cocky attitude. Suddenly, I saw Tommy through Suzette's eyes. Suddenly, I understood that she'd once known the innocence of the little boy who later became the despicable man.

Someone stepped up beside me, and I turned to see Eldon standing there. He pointed to a picture. "That's him and Suzette."

I leaned close to scrutinize the small photo. The tall, ungainly girl stood with her arm wrapped protectively around the little boy with the soulful eyes, whose head reached only to her shoulder. Tears coursed down my cheeks. I thought about the love letters Tommy had written me, the letters I'd thrown away in disgust, and felt ashamed of myself. I wished I'd kept at least one of them as a memento, as a rare expression of tenderness in a seemingly wasted life.

The news of Tommy's death was splashed all over the front page of the local paper, *The Brown County Democrat.* Accompanying the grisly story was a photo of the train that had stopped in a futile effort to avoid running over the inebriated man who'd fallen on the tracks.

People around town talked about the accident with the same fascinated tone they used to discuss a solar eclipse or the birth of a royal baby. They'd take sides over it, some insisting that it was an act of suicide, others arguing that Tommy was too drunk to know what he was doing.

For a week after the article appeared in the paper, nearly every one of my massage clients asked, "Did you hear about that guy who got drunk and walked in front of a train?"

"Yes," I'd say. "He was my friend's nephew. She's really shook up over it."

A look of shock would pass over their faces, as they realized that the unfortunate fellow was part of a family, that he was loved by someone.

I continued to call Eldon every couple of days, asking how his wife was doing. "Not too good," he'd say. "She's still not talking to anybody."

But a week after the funeral, I was surprised when Suzette answered the phone. "How are you?" I asked. "I've been so worried about you."

"I'm coping," she said. "I have to." Her voice sounded strangely calm.

"Could you use some company?"

"Sure, Lanie. Come on over."

When I knocked on the Perrys' front door, Suzette called out in a tremulous voice, "Come in, Lanie." I found her sitting in her recliner, looking like she hadn't moved in days.

I pushed aside the clutter on the sofa and seated myself. "Tell me what happened, Suzette."

She looked at me with tired, empty eyes. "Tommy took his own life." The certainty in her voice surprised me.

"You know that for sure?"

"As sure as I know anything." Wearily, she shifted her position in her chair to face me more directly, as if settling in for a long story. "We were planning to go to his friend Mike's house that evening. Mike and a couple of other guys get together to play country music. I was looking forward to it. I love hearing them play. But at the last minute, Tommy blew up at me. He told me I didn't need to be tagging along with him all the time. He said he'd find another way there.

"That really hurt my feelings. So I stayed home with Eldon that night, and we went to bed early. Then somewhere between midnight and one o'clock, I got a call from Mike's girlfriend, telling me that Tommy was dead. She told me he'd gotten plastered. Then he said he was going to walk home.

Someone offered to drive him, but he insisted on walking. And he walked right in front of that train.

"When I found out, I knew why he'd wanted me out of the way that evening. He had it all planned, and he didn't want me there to stop him. He knew exactly when those trains run through Helmsburg."

"Oh, Suzette," I said. "I feel so bad for you."

"Sometimes, I blame myself for not insisting on going with him," she said, a faraway look in her eyes. "But he was going to do what he was going to do. If it wouldn't have happened that night, it would've been the next night."

"Do you know why he did it?"

"Yes," she said, "I do."

I looked at her questioningly. She hesitated, as if uncertain whether she wanted to divulge Tommy's dark motive.

Then she lowered her eyes, sighing. "I guess I might as well say it, Lanie. Tommy had gotten involved with his friend Steve's sixteen-year-old daughter. Melissa's a little slut. She always had the hots for Tommy, and was always coming on to him. And he took advantage of that. He got her drunk, and they had sex. He was drunk, too, not thinking straight.

"Steve's ex-wife, Melissa's mother, found out about it. She was furious. She's always hated Tommy. She said she was going to press charges. Tommy knew he was going back to prison, and he couldn't face it."

"He told you all that?" I asked.

"Yes, he did. I told you we were close, Lanie. We didn't keep secrets from each other."

A tear spilled from her eye, and she wiped it away with the back of her hand. "Some souls are just too sensitive to live on this earth, Lanie. Life is just too hard for them. Tommy knew he'd come to the end. He'd had enough."

CHAPTER 31

I thought for sure that Tommy's death would settle Suzette down, that she'd give up her rowdy social life and stay home with her husband. I hoped that after her grief subsided, she'd find her way down her basement staircase to her messy studio. I anticipated spending Saturday afternoons with her again. I envisioned sculpting even better figures for her to mold, pieces that would surely sell in all the craft fairs she'd be entering.

But I couldn't have been more wrong. After Tommy's death, something broke loose inside Suzette. Some internal mechanism that held her self-destructive impulses in check gave way completely. Gone was any inhibition, any sense of propriety, any concern about consequences. Her fifty-four-year-old adolescent behavior both baffled and worried me, and I wondered how long her frail body would hold up in the face of this recklessness.

Every time I called the Perrys' house, I'd end up talking to Eldon instead of Suzette. "She's gone out," he'd tell me.

But every now and then, she'd call me back, eager to have an audience for the stories that proved she was still relevant, still desirable, still youthful.

It seemed to me she was hell-bent on keeping Tommy's memory alive by living the life he'd lived, by picking up where he left off. Three weeks after his death, she was back at Frankie's Pub. She became familiar with all the bars in the community, in Morgantown, Trevlac, even as far away as Franklin. She came to know the management of each establishment on a first-name basis. She learned all the sordid details of the lives of the patrons, and conducted her personal counseling sessions in the back booths of each bar.

She'd get out on the dance floor with men twenty years her junior, her legs hurting so badly that she could barely make it through one song. She'd lean up against her partner for support, loving every minute of the intimate contact. Ever the Aphrodite, in a body now plunging madly toward destruction, she'd tell me how difficult it was to resist going home with her dance partner at the end of the evening.

She hung out at Tommy's friend Mike's house whenever he and his buddies got together to drink and play country music. "I could listen to them all night long," she told me. "Mike has the most beautiful singing voice. It's really sexy, just puts me in a trance. If he ever dumps that girlfriend of his, I'll be making a play for him, that's for sure."

She hosted parties at her house, calling me the next morning to complain about the mess she and Eldon had to clean up. In the spring, she returned to the drag-strip, rapidly gathering new people into her burgeoning host of friends.

While I had no desire to accompany her on her escapades, I wondered why she never invited me. I was pretty sure she didn't want any competition for the attention she was getting.

In May, six months after Tommy's death, I got a call from Eldon early on a Sunday morning. "Suzette's in the hospital," he said. "I think she might like a visit from you."

"What happened?" I asked, alarmed.

"She had a heart attack last night."

The news shook me up, but didn't surprise me. After the way she'd been pushing her failing body, a health crisis had been inevitable. "Is it bad?" I asked.

"It wasn't a major heart attack," Eldon said. "But bad enough. The doctor said she needs to change her lifestyle."

"What hospital is she at?"

"Columbus."

"I'll be up to visit later today. Tell her I'll be there."

When I walked into Suzette's hospital room, I found her sitting up in bed wearing an ugly gown, her wispy hair more of a fright than usual. IV tubing was secured to the back of one of her hands. Eldon stood beside the bed, grinning stupidly while his wife barked complaints at her nurse.

"Hi, Suzette," I called.

"Oh, Lanie, I'm so glad to see you," she chortled, reaching out her free hand. "Come sit here with me." I pulled a chair alongside her bed and listened patiently while she recounted every detail of the story surrounding her heart attack.

"I was having a party at the house last night. And wouldn't you know, somebody brought that dude Earl from Trevlac with them. Remember the guy Tommy pushed off the bleachers? I don't know who was stupid enough to think I'd want him in my home. I don't need that kind of shit.

"But there he was, running his goddamn mouth like he always does. I told him to leave. I thought he'd gone, but the next thing I knew, he was back again. He was being a real dick-head, getting under everybody's skin. I don't know how many times I told him to knock off his crap.

"Then he and Greg started getting into it, mouthing off at each other. Earl pushed Greg, and he fell against the fireplace and broke one of the ceramic angels on the mantle. I tell you, Lanie, I was about ready to kill somebody.

"I knew I needed to calm down. So I went outside on the deck to smoke a cigarette."

"A cigarette?" I interrupted. "Suzette, you never used to smoke. When did you start? You know you can't do that with all your health problems."

She grinned sheepishly. "I started about a month ago. I know, I know, I'm a bad girl. But there's so much bullshit going on around me, I have to do something to calm my nerves.

"Anyway, I was out on the deck smoking that cigarette when I started having pains in my chest. Honest to God, Lanie, it felt like I was being crushed, like a three-hundred-pound man was sitting on top of me. I couldn't catch my breath. My knees buckled, and I fell down on the deck and just lay there.

"I yelled, 'Somebody help me!' And would you believe it, none of those selfish jerks would come. I kept yelling and yelling. Finally, Steve's girlfriend came out and said, real snotty-like, 'What do you want?' I said, 'Go find Eldon!'

"Then Eldon called the ambulance, and they brought me here. Honestly, Lanie, if it was up to those idiots, I would've lain there on the deck and died."

"I'm so sorry, Suzette!" I exclaimed. "I hate those people for not helping you when you called. If I would've been there, I would've helped you right away."

She reached over and patted my hand. "I know you would've, Lanie. You're a good friend."

A hospital technician came into the room to inform Suzette that she had an appointment in the radiology department downstairs. She helped Suzette slip on a flimsy hospital robe, and then supported her as she transferred her frail body from the bed to the waiting wheelchair.

"Don't leave yet, Lanie," Suzette said. "This won't take long. Come with me."

The hospital tech led the way, with Eldon following behind her pushing Suzette's IV pole. I brought up the rear of the parade, pushing Suzette in her wheelchair, trying to keep pace with Eldon so as not to stretch the IV tubing too far.

Suzette gathered up the excess tubing in her hand. "Ka-pssshhh, ka-pssshhh," she said, pretending to flog Eldon. He and I both laughed, and the technician turned her head to smile at us. In that moment, I felt rather ordinary in the presence of this homely woman in her frumpy hospital gear, the undisputed queen of the day. I marveled at her ability to make herself the diva of any situation she found herself in.

When we arrived back in Suzette's room, Eldon said, "I think I'll go get some coffee."

"You go right ahead, honey," Suzette said.

As soon as he left the room, she turned to me, scowling. "Thank God, he's finally gone. He's been getting on my nerves all day. I wanted to talk with you alone."

"What about?" I asked.

She closed her eyes for a moment, a blissful smile lighting up her face. "I had a vision, Lanie."

"What do you mean?"

"A vision. You know. You've heard of people having spiritual visions."

"Of course."

She folded her hands primly over the bedcovers and spoke in a hushed voice. "Last night I was sleeping really soundly, better than I had in a long time. Around four o'clock in the morning, something jolted me wide awake. When I opened my eyes, my room was filled with a white glow. There were sparks of light all around me. I knew they were spirits who'd come to help me during my time of need."

"Wow!" I exclaimed.

"They loved me, Lanie. They didn't have to tell me. I could feel it. I was surrounded by all of this wonderful, wonderful love. I never knew love like that existed. I couldn't believe it. All that love, just for me!"

"That's beautiful," I murmured.

Inwardly, I protested. *How does Suzette rate, having a vision like that? The way she's been behaving, she's the last person on earth who deserves one. I've done my best to live a decent life, and nothing like that has ever happened to me.*

Suzette's otherworldly experience reminded me of the meditation room visit with my father, and all my questions that had never been answered. I suddenly wanted to ask Suzette if it was possible to make contact with him again. But I sensed that opportunity had passed, as she was now too caught up in her own drama to be concerned about my life.

She lay back in her bed, smiling serenely, holding her palms up as if in communion with the divine. Her frizzy hair splayed out on the pillow, surrounding her head like a halo. "God is so good to me," she whispered.

A minute later, she was complaining again. "My doctor said I have to stay here at least another three days. He needs to make sure my blood pressure is stable, and he wants to start me on a strict diabetic diet plan. He's sending some damn dietician up here to talk to me. I told him he's wasting his time. He knows I'll never stick to any diet they put me on."

CHAPTER 32

I desperately hoped Suzette's health crisis would serve as her much-needed wake-up call. Something as serious as a heart attack was bound to bring her to her senses. I pictured her shooing the party riff-raff out of her house and settling down to a quiet life with Eldon. After having had a vision, she'd certainly want to focus on her spiritual life again. Surely, she'd clear Tommy's mess out of her meditation room and reinstate her altar.

But Suzette had a different idea of what to do with her sense of time running out. She was determined to pack in all the life she could, in the way she saw fit to live it.

After she left the hospital, I didn't hear from Suzette for two months. When I'd call her house, no one would answer the phone. I wondered why I didn't even hear Eldon's voice on the other end of the line.

When I finally caught up with her, Suzette acted surprised that I hadn't heard she was divorcing her husband. "Didn't I tell you, Lanie?" she said. "I finally worked up the nerve to kick that slug out of my house and out of my life." She sounded proud, like she'd just accomplished something on her bucket list.

"Where did Eldon go?" I asked.

"He moved into an apartment. I don't know where, and I don't care. I'm done with him."

Oh, Suzette, what have you done? I protested inwardly. *Eldon is your meal ticket. He keeps a roof over your head. He buys your insulin. He helps you up the stairs when you're too weak to make it on your own. And he's been at your side through all the rough times: Tommy's death, your heart attack.*

"I've got someone else in my life," she said, sounding like a schoolgirl divulging a juicy secret.

I tried to keep the sarcasm out of my response. "Are you serious?"

"Oh yes, Lanie. His name is Jerry. I met him at the racetrack. We hit it off right away. We sat there for hours on the bleachers, just talking and getting to know each other. And then we started developing feelings for each other."

She paused, as if waiting for me to congratulate her, but I was too stunned to say anything. Then she continued.

"I said to Jerry, 'What are we going to do about these feelings?' And we decided he'd move in with me."

"How are you going to pay your bills?" I asked when I finally found my voice.

"Jerry's on Social Security," she said nonchalantly. "He told me he'd put his check toward my house payment. And I have some extra bedrooms, two upstairs and the one in the basement where Tommy slept. I can always take in boarders if I get behind on bills. It'll work out, Lanie."

"I sure hope so," I said.

"I want you to meet Jerry. Why don't you come over this evening?"

I was hoping for the best. I really was. I wanted to meet a kindly gentleman who would deliver that elusive magical essence Suzette longed for in a lover. But when I knocked on her door, I heard a chilling male voice shouting ugly obscenities at the barking Chihuahua. I dislike Suzette's new boyfriend before I even laid eyes on him.

Good Lord, Suzette! I thought when he flung open the door. *This man makes Eldon look like Prince Charming.*

It seemed to me that she'd picked an older version of

Tommy Crawford, twenty years ahead in the drinking game. Jerry's bulging belly looked uncomfortably out of place on his otherwise scrawny frame, like a python that had just swallowed a watermelon-sized rat. His ruddy, deeply-creased face sported a stubble of whiskers, and both his skin and his hair appeared oily and unwashed. He reeked of cigarette smoke. His grimy blue jeans rode low on his skinny hips to accommodate his belly, and his dingy tee shirt exposed the old, faded tattoos on his forearms. His bleary eyes peered at me suspiciously.

"I'm Suzette's friend," I informed him.

Jerry turned his head and bellowed over his shoulder. "Suzette! There's somebody here to see you!"

Suzette hurried out of the kitchen, smiling from ear to ear. "Lanie, this is Jerry," she said as graciously as if she was introducing me to the Prince of Wales. "Jerry, this is my friend Lanie."

"Pleased to meet you," I said, reluctantly extending my hand.

Jerry nodded and grunted, ignoring my invitation for a handshake. Then he pulled a cigarette from the pack in his shirt pocket, lit it, and shuffled out of the room.

I glanced around, trying to hide my dismay. Suzette's usual cluttered ambiance had degenerated into grime and filth. She gestured for me to sit down on the sofa, which was spotted with grease stains, food spills, and dog hair. Suddenly, I understood the reason for the squalor. Good old Eldon was no longer around to run the vacuum cleaner or shampoo the furniture. Suzette didn't have the energy for those tasks, and Jerry clearly wasn't oriented toward cleanliness.

My gaze fell on the clutter of beer bottles on the coffee

table. "Jerry doesn't drink hard liquor anymore," Suzette announced proudly. "I won't let him." She shot me a smug look that said, *See? I have everything under control.*

The stench in the house was so overpowering that I could hardly listen as Suzette rambled on about what she and Jerry had been doing, places they'd gone, and who'd been at the house for parties. After twenty minutes, I apologized and told her I had somewhere else to go.

"Stop by any time, Lanie," she called after me as I walked out the door.

As summer moved into autumn, Suzette filled her spare rooms with boarders she'd found through her network of sordid connections. The first to come were Butch and Larry.

"Butch is working now," she told me. "Larry doesn't have a job. Nobody would hire anyone that stupid. But I told them they could live here two for the price of one if they shared a room."

Several days after Butch and Larry moved in, Suzette called me to complain about their behavior. "Those boys eat like hogs," she groused. "Food is so expensive now. Jerry and I went grocery shopping a couple of days ago. It took two hundred bucks just to fill up one cart. And it's almost gone now. I bought a bag of chips for Jerry and me to snack on while we watch TV. It came up missing, and I found the empty bag in the boys' room. And Butch has been getting into Jerry's beer. That really pisses Jerry off. He started hollering at Butch last night. Butch hollered back, and I had to tell both of them to shut up."

Four weeks later, Butch went to jail after getting into a bar fight. Suzette couldn't keep Larry free of charge, and told him he had to leave.

"They ate me out of house and home," she complained bitterly. "And I didn't get a dime of rent out of them. Now I've got all their crap upstairs, and I don't know what to do with it. Bag it up and throw it in the trash, I suppose."

In spite of her badgering, Jerry refused to hand over even one Social Security check, so after three months, Suzette told him to hit the road. Within two weeks, she moved in a second alcoholic boyfriend, but threw him out a month later because he gave her too much attitude.

She didn't fare any better with subsequent boarders. They all made promises they never intended to keep, taking more from her than they gave. When one would go to jail or skip town without paying her a nickel, she'd find another desperate soul to take his place.

"Someday, it'll all work out," she told me. "Someday, I'll find the right combination of people, and we'll live together in peace. These things take time, Lanie."

But no matter whom she had under her roof, her boarders fought with each other, driving Suzette to the brink of insanity. They brought in their indigent friends as houseguests, and soon all three levels of Suzette's home were littered with indolent bodies.

One day, she told me how one of the young men sneaked up behind her while she was standing at the kitchen sink and poked her in the ribs. "He scared the living daylights out of me," she said. "Almost gave me another heart attack."

So she grabbed a skillet off the stove and swung at him, landing some heavy blows on his head and shoulders. He didn't give her any trouble for the rest of the day. "You have to do this to keep men in line, Lanie," she said, as if instructing me in the fine art of relationship maintenance. "Otherwise, they won't listen to you."

By the time winter arrived, Suzette was seriously behind on her mortgage payments, and was unable to come up with money for her mounting utility bills. "The gas company's threatening to turn off our heat!" she wailed over the phone one day. "It's friggin' cold outside! We're going to freeze to death! I've got to get some money coming into the house. I've got to get back to working on my business. Will you sculpt something for me, Lanie?"

I knew the few dollars that would come through selling her crafts wouldn't make a dent in Suzette's rapidly increasing debt. But I said, "Sure. Want me to continue with the line of dog breeds?"

"Anything, Lanie!" she begged. "Anything!"

CHAPTER 33

The following week, I dedicated my spare time to sculpting a golden retriever and a basset hound. Even though the figures turned out beautifully, I felt depressed. I knew my effort to help Suzette was an exercise in futility.

On a snowy January morning, I drove to Helmsburg, and then turned onto the narrow, slippery Lick Creek Road. When I saw that Suzette's steep driveway was covered with a foot of snow, I knew I couldn't take the risk of trying to drive all the way up to her house. So I parked my car alongside the road, hoping there wouldn't be much traffic passing by during the few minutes I planned to stay there.

Carrying the box in which I'd packed my dog sculptures, I trudged up the driveway through the drifts. I suddenly realized Suzette was virtually trapped in her home, completely snowbound. If Eldon had been living there, he would have taken charge of snow removal. I wondered why she hadn't persuaded one of her boarders to do some shoveling. There had to be an able-bodied man among the lot.

I stood on her ice-covered steps, hesitating to knock, not wanting to face what was inside. I could hear scuffling and swearing, and several minutes passed before Suzette opened the door. She looked frazzled, her face dark with anger.

"Come on in, Lanie," she muttered.

The foul odor in the house hit me like a tidal wave, making me nauseous. The filth and clutter were even more overwhelming than on my visit five months earlier.

An elderly man sat on Suzette's stained sofa, looking as if he'd grown up out of the rubbish. His frame was hunched and emaciated, the only fat on his body having lodged in his little pot belly. His grizzled, unshaven face was slack and expressionless, his eyes cloudy and vacant. From ten feet away, I smelled the stench of alcohol oozing from his pores.

You've got to get out of here, I told myself. *Just give Suzette the sculptures and run.*

"I brought these for you," I said, holding out my box. "I made you a golden retriever and a basset hound."

"Just put them over there for now." Suzette gestured toward the dining room table, which was laden with dirty dishes, a crumpled newspaper, several cereal boxes, beer bottles and soda cans, an open bag of chips, and a single scuffed sneaker. I glanced around and saw the matching sneaker lying just inside the kitchen doorway.

I was reluctant to deposit my treasure in the middle of the mess, but I obligingly pushed some of the empty cans aside to clear a space for my box.

"Have a seat," Suzette said irritably. "I'm in the middle of something right now."

I looked around at my choice of seats, all of which were littered and stained with filth, and decided I'd prefer to stand. "That's okay," I said. "I can only stay a minute."

Scowling, Suzette marched over to the stairwell leading to the upstairs bedrooms. "Brandon, I told you to get that thing out of here!" she yelled. "And I mean now!"

"Okay, okay!" a voice shouted back. "Just give me a minute."

"I gave you a minute half an hour ago. Now get a move on it!"

A moment later, a young man wearing an overcoat and pajama bottoms clattered down the stairs, carrying a battered cardboard box. Suzette peered into the box, and then recoiled. "Now get it out of here. And if you even think of bringing another one in, I'll beat your brains out."

As the young man carried the box through the living room and out the front door, she yelled, "Take it out and throw it in the creek. Just bust the ice and dump it in."

"No, Aunt Susie!" Brandon protested. "It'll freeze to death."

"I don't give a rat's ass if it freezes," she screamed at him. "Just get it out of here."

"What the heck's going on?" I asked her.

She shook her head in disgust. "That stupid kid brought his pet hognose snake with him when he moved in here last month. I didn't even know he had it until another guy told me this morning." She shuddered. "He was taking that damn thing out and letting it slither all over his room. Last thing I need is to have my house infested with snakes."

I heard footsteps coming up the basement stairs, and another young man, barefoot and tousle-haired, walked into the living room. His shirtless torso was well-formed and muscular, and mischievous blue eyes sparkled in his handsome face.

He sauntered over to Suzette and kissed her on the cheek. "Good morning, Aunt Susie."

She shoved him away, smiling. "Get off me, Chad."

"Are you going to the store today?"

"Now, how do you think I'm supposed to do that, with all this snow? I'll go tomorrow, if I can get out."

"Remember what I asked you to get?"

"Yes, I remember, but I didn't promise you anything. Now would you get your filthy shoes off my dining room table?"

Grinning, he walked over to the table and picked up the single sneaker. "Where's the other one, Aunt Susie?"

"How the hell should I know?" she retorted.

"It's in the kitchen," I said.

The young man looked my way, flashing me a seductive smile. "Who's your hot friend, Aunt Susie?"

"Never you mind," she snapped. "She's not interested in you, you little tomcat, so don't you go sniffin' around her."

She smiled fondly as she watched the young man head back downstairs. "That damn kid is always buttering me up, trying to get what he wants. He's too cute for his own good."

Then her gaze fell on the old man sitting on the sofa. "Did you get any breakfast, Clifford?"

He slowly turned his head and fixed his bleary eyes on her. "Huh?"

"Did you get any breakfast?"

"I don't think so," he mumbled.

"I'll fix you something in a minute. We've got to get something inside you besides all that booze. You're getting way too skinny."

She turned to me. "This man has three daughters, and not a one of them will have him in her house. Can you imagine treating your dad like that?"

"I really need to go," I said.

Suzette sighed. "Sorry, Lanie. Maybe some other time we'll have a chance to visit."

I waited three weeks for Suzette to mold the dog sculptures. I finally called to see how they were coming along.

"I tried," she said, "but the molds didn't turn out right. I'm just too nervous with . . ."

I finished the sentence I'd heard her say a hundred times before. ". . . all that bullshit going on around you."

"You've got that right, Lanie. It's crazy around here."

After I hung up the phone, I flopped down on my sofa, feeling heavy and dejected. I knew my involvement with Suzette and her business was over. She'd completely lost her grip on her work. Nothing creative was ever going to come out of that messy basement studio again.

Tears spilled from my eyes as I thought back over the three-and-a-half years I'd known Suzette. She'd loved me, comforted me, guided me, and even protected me. She'd been like a mother to me, venturing with me into places my own timid mother couldn't take me. But now my gritty, outrageous surrogate mother had lost her way and was teetering on the verge of self-destruction.

There's nothing more you can do, I reminded myself for the umpteenth time. *She's living her life the way she wants to. There's no room for you in it anymore. Just leave her be. You've got plenty going on in your own life.*

I had enough to focus on. My massage business was doing very well. I'd been thinking about going back to school to get further training, to add something fresh to my work.

I was almost finished with a sculpture that Margaret Brown had praised profusely: an angel reclining on a rock surrounded by wildflowers, lovingly petting a fox that had snuggled up to her. Margaret said the sculpture embodied Brown County's spirit of nature, and she wanted me to place it in her gallery.

I have to keep moving ahead, I thought. *Even if Suzette doesn't.*

CHAPTER 34

The rest of that winter, I immersed myself in my projects at the studio. While snowfall blanketed my outer world, I savored my inner serenity and the thrill of new creation. But in April, Suzette yanked me back into chaos when she called with tragic news. "Lanie," she whimpered. "I'm losing my home. What am I going to do?"

Oh God, I thought. *I knew it would come to this.*

"I'm so sorry, Suzette," I said. "I wish I knew what to tell you. Have you tried going anywhere to get help?"

"I don't know where to go," she wailed.

I wracked my brain for ideas. "Why don't you start with the Welfare Department? I don't know if they can help you, but they might be able to tell you some place that can."

"Okay, I'll try that. Thank you, Lanie."

Then I heard a crash in the background, followed by swearing. The desperation in Suzette's voice changed to her usual tone of irritation. "Gotta go, Lanie. There's all kinds of hell breaking loose around here. Those goddamn boys! I'm gonna have to knock a few heads together."

This isn't your problem, I told myself as I hung up the phone. *Suzette has to deal with the consequences of her own choices.* I picked up my car keys, ready to head off to the studio, but put them down again. Deeply resenting the disruption of my peaceful schedule, I sat down at my computer, where I spent an hour on the internet, researching organizations that provide assistance to people on the verge of homelessness.

With list of resources in hand, I reached for the phone, ready to dial Suzette's number. Then I stopped. Grimacing, I forced myself to consider an obvious solution: Suzette could share my home until she got back on her feet.

That's a terrible idea, I argued with myself. *Having a business in this tiny house doesn't leave room for a second occupant. Suzette can't share a bedroom with me, because she wouldn't able to manage the stairs. And I couldn't have her sleeping in the living room with clients coming in and out of the house.*

But I knew if I was the one who was homeless, Suzette would invite me to sleep on her sofa, without questioning whether I was deserving of her charity.

Taking a deep breath to shore up my resolve, I reached for the phone again. "Suzette," I said when she answered, "why don't you come stay with me for awhile?"

After a long silence, she said, "Lanie, I appreciate your offer. You're such a kind person, and I know you care about me. But I can't barge in on your life like that. Remember what I told you the first time I came to your house?"

"What are you talking about?" I asked.

"I told you I hoped nothing would ever enter your home that would disturb your peace. And I really meant that. If I moved in with you, I'd be bringing a lot of problems with me. My life is a mess right now. You've got some great things going on in your life, and I'd just drag you down. Lanie, I love you way too much to do that to you. Don't worry about me. I'll figure something out."

Even though I sensed Suzette wanted me to leave her alone, I called her once a week to check on her. She never answered her phone.

When she finally returned my calls six weeks later, she was in a cheerful mood. "God is looking out for me, Lanie. Everything's going to be okay. I got signed up for disability benefits, and tomorrow, I'm moving into a government-subsidized apartment."

A wave of relief washed over me. "Oh, Suzette, that's wonderful! I'm so glad for you."

"I'm so amazed at how everything worked out," she said. "I made a few bucks from selling some of my furniture. That will help get me started in my new place. My car broke down, but it was just a heap of junk, and I didn't have enough money to get it fixed. So I told myself I didn't need a car anymore, and I sold it for scrap parts."

"What's happening with all your boarders?" I asked. "I hope you're not taking any of them with you."

"Hell, no!" she exclaimed. "I got rid of all of those idiots a month ago. When I found out for sure that I was going to lose this house, I decided I was going to spend my last few weeks here in peace and quiet. So I told all the guys they had to hit the road. A couple of them refused to budge, and I had to call the sheriff's department to get them out."

"So you've been all alone out there? With no car to go anywhere?"

"Yup. I've spent every day sitting on the deck, looking out into the woods, just soaking up the beauty of nature. My friend Shirley brought me groceries a couple of times."

"Who's Shirley?" I asked.

"She's someone I met at the drag-strip. She's a real nice gal. Has a heart of gold. She's helped me out a lot."

A surge of old jealousy darkened my mood. *Why didn't Suzette ask me for help? Why wasn't I the one carrying bags of groceries to her? She's probably all wrapped up with Shirley, like she was with Tommy before he died. Like she was with me before that. I don't mean anything to her anymore.*

No sooner had I indulged in that little pout than wiser thoughts alighted in my mind. *Come on, Elaine, you've moved past all Suzette's drama. You know that, and she knows that. She respects that. Even though her life is sliding downhill, she wants you to soar. She's pushed you out of her life because she cares about you.*

"Nope, I haven't minded being alone at all," Suzette mused. "These have been some of the best weeks of my life." Then her voice took on a mischievous tone. "But I'm not going to be alone tonight."

"Oh?" I said. "What's happening?"

"Today's my birthday. Shirley asked me what I wanted for a birthday present. I told her I wanted to spend my last evening in my home with a man. You know, sit in front of the fireplace, light some candles, put on romantic music, drink a little wine, and see where things go from there.

"Lanie, I was just talking out of my ass. I didn't think there was any chance my wish was going to come true. But you know what? Shirley's bringing her brother over here for me tonight. I've never met this guy, but I know in my heart we're going to hit it off. God is so good to me!"

I was glad Suzette couldn't see me at the other end of the line, shaking my head in disgust. I tried not to imagine the caliber of man who'd end up in her bed that night. "Well, I hope you have a nice time," I told her.

"I gotta go, Lanie," she said. "I've got so much to do to get ready for tonight."

"Will you have the same phone number after you move?"

"I don't think so," she said. "I'll call you with my new number after I get my phone service hooked up."

She didn't call me, and I wasn't surprised. I told myself that she was okay, that she was safe and secure in her new residence. But I couldn't shake off a feeling of uneasiness, a sense of impending doom. *Something's wrong with Suzette,* I told myself. *Something's terribly wrong.*

I called her old number, only to hear a recording that said it was no longer in service. So I resorted to using Directory Assistance to obtain her new number. When she answered the phone, she sounded weak and exhausted.

"I'm so glad I found you!" I exclaimed. "How are you doing, Suzette? How do you like your new home?"

"My new home is fine." It sounded like it took all of her strength to utter those words.

"What's wrong?"

"Lanie, I'm so tired these days. My doctor told me my kidneys are failing. He's got me running to dialysis three times a week. They come pick me up in a van and drive me to Columbus. It's exhausting."

"Oh my God, Suzette! I'm so sorry. How do you manage living on your own? Who's looking after you?"

"My doctor got me signed up for home health care. The ladies come in several times a week. They do my housework and laundry. I have Meals on Wheels bringing me food. Don't worry, Lanie. I'm being taken care of."

I felt a powerful urge to rush to her side. "Can I come see you?" I asked.

"No, sweetie," she said. "I'm just too tired. I don't have the strength to talk with people anymore."

"I understand," I mumbled, feeling profoundly rejected.

"I still love you, honey," she whispered.

I knew Suzette had completely closed the door on our friendship. I knew I would never see or speak to her again. I hung up the telephone and cried.

In my mind's eye, I severed the cord that had held our relationship together, the once-strong bond that had grown weak and frayed. It was over.

CHAPTER 35

As the months passed, my life continued to move in directions far from the world I'd shared with Suzette. One day a week, I drove to my former school in Indianapolis, first, to take post-graduate courses in massage therapy, and later, classes in energy healing. These advanced levels of training enthralled me, opening doors to learning experiences I'd never conceived of, teaching me skills I'd never dreamed I could master. Sometimes, I'd stare at my reflection in the mirror, trying to comprehend the fact that I was no longer the meek and mousy girl I'd thought I'd always be. Elaine Greene had become a highly competent professional woman.

Under Margaret Brown's tutelage, I'd continued to hone my skills as a sculptor. I'd accumulated a sizable collection of work, and Margaret told me I was almost ready for a personal show at her gallery.

While I had little time for dating, I'd caught the attention of a few interesting men. However, none of them impressed me as a suitable partner for a long-term relationship.

Sometimes as I lay in bed at night, my thoughts would drift back to Suzette. I'd wish that I could tell her about the new developments in my life. *I told you, Lanie,* I could almost hear her say. *You're moving on to bigger and better things.*

When she'd first said those words, I'd felt rejected. Now, I realized she'd known the ways in which I needed to grow.

One morning in October, the phone rang while I was getting ready for my day's work. As I was feeling rushed, my first inclination was to let the call go through to the answering machine. But something prompted me to pick up the receiver.

"I'm a nurse at the Senior Health and Living Community," the caller said.

That's a nursing home in Nashville, I told myself.

"I'm trying to locate the family of Virginia Harding. Are you a relative?"

"No," I said, "I'm not."

"Do you happen to know any of her family members?"

"No. I don't know Virginia Harding. You must've dialed the wrong number."

"I'm sorry for bothering you," the nurse said.

But in a split second, a rush of thoughts slammed into my mind and sorted themselves out. Suzette's legal name was Virginia. I'd forgotten that. Her maiden name was Harding. She must have taken it back when she divorced Eldon. My friend whom I'd only known as Suzette Perry was once again Virginia Harding.

"Wait!" I said to the caller who was ready to hang up. "I know who you're talking about."

The nurse breathed a sigh of relief. "Oh, good! We have no contact information whatsoever on Virginia here at the nursing home."

Seriously? I thought. *Suzette was admitted to a nursing home and none of her five brothers showed up on the scene? Didn't they care enough about their sister to keep track of her? Those sons-of-bitches!*

Hadn't any of the friends she'd made at the bars and the racetrack proven to be reliable? Hadn't any of her boarders stepped up and become someone she could count on? Or had she finally become so sick and tired of all the bullshit going on around her that she'd shut everyone out, like she had me?

"We found an old phone book in Virginia's possession," the nurse said. "Your name and number were written in the back of it. That was the only lead we could find."

Alarm bells rang in my head. I knew something was terribly wrong. Suzette was gravely ill, probably at death's door. There could be no other reason for the nurse's call.

"How is she?" I asked, frantic.

"I'm not allowed to give out information about her condition," the nurse said. "But I can tell you she was just taken by ambulance to Columbus Regional Hospital."

"Can I see her there?"

"Of course you can. But you'll need to hurry. She'll be on the third floor."

As quickly as I could, I called the clients on my schedule for the day to cancel their appointments. Then I jumped into my car for the thirty minute drive to Columbus Hospital. *Please, God,* I prayed, *just let me make it to the hospital before she dies. She needs me there with her.*

It seemed like everyone in the world had come to Brown County to see the autumn colors, and the tourist traffic through Nashville moved at a snail's pace. I pounded my steering wheel in frustration. *God, I've got to get there in time. Make this traffic move!*

After an interminable crawl through town, I finally turned east onto State Road 46 and headed toward Columbus. Picking up speed, I breathed a sigh of relief. *Hold on, Suzette. I'm coming. I'll be there for you.*

When I reached the Columbus city limits, the traffic lights began to slow me down. Each stop felt like wasted moments. *Please, God, let me get to the hospital before she dies!*

Finding a spot in the hospital parking garage and riding the elevator to the third floor seemed to take forever. But I finally arrived at the nurses' station, exhausted and out of breath.

"Could you tell me Virginia Harding's room number?" I asked the nurse who was seated at the desk.

"Virginia is downstairs getting some tests done," she said. Then she looked up at me, a hopeful expression on her face. "Are you a family member?"

"No, I'm her friend."

"Well, thank God someone showed up for her. We don't have any contact information on Virginia. The nursing home wasn't able to give us anything. Do you know how to reach any of her family members?"

"I know she has brothers," I said. "But I don't know any of them personally." I wracked my brain for their names, but the only one I could come up with was Tommy Crawford's stepfather. "The only name I remember is Oscar. Oscar Harding. I don't know his number, and I have no idea where he lives. Possibly somewhere in Morgantown."

"Thank you," the nurse said. "I'll try to locate him. And I'll let you know when Virginia comes back upstairs. You can go to the waiting room. I'll show you where it is." She got up from her desk and walked me down the hallway.

I sat in the large, crowded waiting room, talking to Suzette in my mind. *I'm here, Suzette. Hang on, please hang on. I'll be with you in a few minutes.*

CHAPTER 36

Twenty minutes later, the nurse beckoned to me from the doorway of the waiting room. A man in a dark suit stood beside her. I got up and walked toward them, eager for news about Suzette.

"This is Reverend Simons," the nurse said. "He's the hospital chaplain."

The implications of the chaplain's presence didn't immediately register with me.

"Virginia passed away before she made it back upstairs," the nurse continued. "We've cleaned up her body. You can spend some time with her now."

The kindly chaplain put his arm around my shoulders and guided me to Suzette's room. A hundred thoughts raced through my mind during that short walk.

I can't believe it. Suzette's gone.

God, I prayed to get to the hospital before she died. I was here, but I wasn't with her. Didn't you understand what I meant? Couldn't you have allowed me a few minutes at her bedside?

I'm the only one here for her. Where is her family? Where are all those friends whose company she preferred to mine? Was nobody around during her last days? Did she think she was dying alone? That would have been so awful for her!

But maybe she chose to spend her last days in solitude.

The nurse and chaplain seem to think I'm in charge here. Are they expecting me to make arrangements? I have no idea what to do. This is supposed to be a family matter.

God, I'm so glad it's ME that's here. It was no accident that the nurse found MY number in Suzette's phone book. This was meant to be. Whether Suzette knew it or not, I was the truest friend she had, the only one she could really count on.

"I'll let you spend some time alone with her," Reverend Simons said in a consoling voice. "If there's anything I can do, please let me know." He gazed at me with compassion in his eyes, as if I was the primary bereaved party.

Taking a deep breath, I walked into the room and approached the body lying on the bed. *This isn't Suzette,* I thought. The hollow-cheeked old woman with her mouth agape had nothing to do with the friend I'd known.

The bedcovers were neatly drawn up to her chin, covering her arms and hands. The body appeared suspiciously short under the blankets, and a feeling of dread crept over me. I touched the bed where her legs should have been, and the blanket collapsed beneath the weight of my hand.

Suzette's long, slender legs had finally succumbed to the advancement of her diabetes and had been amputated. The legs that had painfully made their way down the staircase to her basement studio. The legs that had tried in vain to climb the bleachers at the racetrack. The legs that had danced in bars for as long as they possibly could. They were gone. I wondered how long she'd been without them, and how she'd adjusted to the loss of them.

Still, my mind wasn't fully convinced that this body was Suzette's. I knew what I needed to do to prove it to myself. Ever so discreetly, I lifted the covers off the hand nearest me.

Without a doubt, it was Suzette's large, elegant, long-fingered hand, the hand I'd watched moving delicately over my sculptures, the hand I'd watched gesturing theatrically while she told her outrageous stories. But the nails were rough and broken, with only traces of her signature pink polish. She'd been unable to keep up with them at the end.

I carefully lifted the hand and held it between the two of mine. It felt cold, completely devoid of Suzette's life.

I didn't know how far away her spirit had traveled, but I hoped it was hovering near enough to hear me speak. I thanked her for the time we'd spent together in her studio, for the confidence she'd shown in my sculpting. I thanked her for pushing me, even when I didn't want to be pushed. I thanked her for the enchanting candlelit hours at her velvet-shrouded alter, for her stories, for her prayers, for her love.

The nurse appeared in the doorway. "I'm so sorry to interrupt you, but I can't locate Oscar Harding. Do you have any more leads?"

I shook my head. "No, I don't." *Oh, dear God,* I thought. *What happens if no one steps up and makes arrangements for Suzette's body? Will she be given a pauper's burial?*

Suddenly, I remembered someone I hadn't thought about in several years: Eldon's son Kenneth Perry. Suzette had been so proud of her stepson because he worked at Columbus Hospital. Kenneth could contact his father, who would surely have information about Suzette's brothers.

"Does Kenneth Perry still work here?" I asked the nurse.

"Ken Perry from I. T.? Yes, he works here. He was just up here this morning fixing my computer."

Of course, I thought. *He'd go by Ken, not Kenneth.*

"He knew Virginia," I said. "She used to be his stepmother. He might be able to get you some information about her family."

The nurse breathed a sigh of relief. "Thank you. I'll page him right away."

Within minutes, I saw a familiar slim, balding figure in khaki trousers standing at the nurses' station. The nurse said a few words to him, and then pointed to the room where I was holding vigil with Suzette's body.

When Ken walked into the room and saw the body on the bed, a look of shock replaced his expression of cool composure. I was so happy to see him, so glad to have someone to brave this crisis with me that I wanted to run across the room and throw my arms around him.

"I remember you," he said. "You're Lanie Greene. You were at my dad's house for Thanksgiving several years ago."

"Yes," I said. "That was me."

He gestured toward the bed. "What happened?"

"I don't have a lot to tell you. I hadn't seen Suzette in months." I realized I'd made myself sound like a bad friend, so I hurriedly came to my own defense. "I wanted to visit her, but she kept brushing me off."

Ken nodded. "She was a moody person."

Then I told him the story about the nurse finding my name in the back of Suzette's phonebook. "So here I am. I was afraid no one else would show up. The hospital doesn't have any contact information on her family. I figured your dad might be able to help."

"Good thinking," he said. "I'll call him."

He turned abruptly and left the room. I watched him stop at the nurse's desk and say something to her. She handed him the phone.

While he talked, he jotted notes on a piece of paper. After handing the paper to the nurse, he walked away, disappearing from my sight. I felt a twinge of sadness at his departure.

What do I do now? I wondered. As I gazed at Suzette's body, I knew I couldn't bear leaving her alone. *I guess I'll just wait until someone else gets here.*

A few minutes later, the nurse stood in the doorway again. "I was able to locate one of Virginia's brothers. He's on his way."

Half an hour passed before a tall man around sixty years of age walked into the room. I recognized some of Suzette's features in his face, the owlish eyes and the strong jaw line. He looked disgruntled, as if he resented the fact that his sister's death had interrupted his afternoon nap.

"Who are you?" he asked rather rudely.

"I'm Lanie Greene." I realized that, for the first time, I'd introduced myself by Suzette's pet name for me. "I'm Suzette's friend."

"I'm Harold Harding," he said gruffly. He looked at his sister's body lying on the bed. "I hadn't seen her in awhile. I didn't know she was that bad off."

I clenched my jaw to keep from saying something decidedly unfriendly.

"What am I supposed to do?" he asked. The irritation in his voice revealed his underlying attitude: *why is all this on me?*

I wanted to run over and slap his ugly face. Instead, I said, "Well, you need to contact the rest of the family. Then you need to arrange something with a funeral home. The nurses will help you."

I bent down to kiss Suzette's cold cheek, whispering my final goodbye before reluctantly leaving her in the hands of her uncaring brother.

On my drive home, I noticed that my hands were trembling on the steering wheel. By the time I reached Nashville, my entire body was shaking, my teeth chattering. When I pulled into my driveway, the shaking intensified to convulsive proportions. I was barely able to walk into my house, and when I finally made it inside, I collapsed on my sofa and wept.

CHAPTER 37

When I didn't see Suzette's obituary in *The Brown County Democrat,* I checked with the Bowen-Marshall Funeral Home in Nashville to see if arrangements had been made there. Nothing had been scheduled for Virginia Harding.

Aren't those horrible brothers even holding a service for her? I fumed. *Aren't they going to acknowledge their sister's life and death in any manner?*

Then it occurred to me that arrangements might have been made in Suzette's hometown. I checked with the Madison-Cooper Funeral Home in Morgantown, and sure enough, her service had been scheduled for the upcoming Friday evening. Perhaps those brothers had a bit of decency after all.

I dreaded the thought of attending the funeral. I knew I'd be going through an emotionally draining experience, alone in a crowd of strangers. So on Thursday afternoon, I stopped at the National City Bank to talk with my mother.

"Do you remember me telling you about my friend Suzette?" I asked her.

"The one you sculpted for?"

"Yes. She passed away last week."

Then I recounted the bizarre circumstances that had led me to the hospital on the day of Suzette's death. "Her funeral is tomorrow evening," I said. "I know I'm being silly, Mom, but I don't want to go alone. Will you come with me?"

Her face lit up at my request. "Of course I'll go with you, honey. You've been through so much already. You shouldn't have to go through any more of this ordeal without some support. I'll pick you up and drive you there."

The next evening, we drove to Morgantown and pulled into the parking lot of the Madison-Cooper Funeral Home. As we walked toward the entrance of the long brick building, my mother reached over and took my hand. It reminded me of the way she'd led me down the sidewalks of Nashville when I was a tiny child, one of the rare times she was allowed to assert her motherly rights.

I was disappointed when we entered the room where Suzette's service was to be held. It was nearly empty. Half a dozen rows of chairs had been set up, but few of them were occupied. Five elderly men, undoubtedly Suzette's brothers, sat in the front two rows, accompanied by women I assumed to be their wives. Several of the brothers appeared frail, and one of them was seated in a wheelchair. I wondered how these old men had all managed to outlive their younger sister.

There was no casket, so I figured Suzette's remains had been cremated. There were no pictures displayed, no memorabilia of her life. A single, modest bouquet of chrysanthemums stood beside the podium where the minister was to deliver his eulogy. The brothers certainly hadn't outdone themselves.

I looked for familiar faces in the handful of people scattered here and there on the rest of the chairs. Was Eldon here? I desperately wanted to hear his goofy voice singing out, "Hi, Lanie." Today, his trademark lingering hug would have been comforting rather than annoying. But I didn't spot him in the sparse crowd. He and Suzette had been divorced for more than a year, and after the way she'd treated him, I didn't blame him for not showing up.

How about Jerry, her old boyfriend? Her so-called nephews, Butch and Larry? Brandon the snake boy? Chad the charmer? Old Clifford? None of them were present to honor the memory of the woman who had once been significant in their lives.

The minister stood up to offer a few words of inspiration, his voice dripping with well-practiced sentimentality. Midway through his speech, I heard a disturbance in the back of the room. When I looked over my shoulder, I saw a dozen disheveled people straggling in, bringing with them the stench of alcohol that settled over the room like a cloud of despair.

Suzette's bar friends? Maybe some of the people she counseled from her office in the back booth? I was glad they'd come, glad they at least took up a few more of the empty chairs.

One of the brothers glanced around at the newcomers, then nudged the brother sitting next to him and whispered a few words. The two of them exchanged self-righteous smirks. I was so angry that I felt like pummeling them. I squeezed my fists hard in an effort to contain my fury, my nails digging into my palms.

After the minister concluded his short sermon, he invited Suzette's loved ones to speak. For a few minutes, the room remained so silent that I could hear the asthmatic breathing of the brother in the wheelchair. Finally, one of the other rickety brothers struggled to his feet, leaning heavily on his cane.

"I guess it's time to share our memories," he said. "We all loved our sister, and we tried our best to look out for her. At times like this, it's tempting to glorify the life of the person who has departed. But let's not pretend here. Let's not make Virginia out to be someone she wasn't."

He continued speaking for half a minute, but I didn't hear the rest of what he said, because I was fuming.

Then another brother stood up. "Virginia was a person with big ideas," he said. "Unfortunately, most of them never amounted to anything. She had a hard time facing life as it was. She preferred living in her own little fantasy world. She couldn't even live with her given name. When she came back home from California, she insisted on being called Suzette. That's something we never got used to."

"Virginia was strong-willed, I'll give her that," another brother said. "She never backed down from anybody. She could be hard to deal with. Everything had to be her way or no way."

How could you guys say all this crap about your sister? I seethed. *How could you not know who she really was? How dare you memorialize her as if she was nothing more than a nuisance to you?*

I glanced around to see if anyone else was on the verge of speaking. The bar friends maintained their silent stupor, not a sniffle among them.

Well, I told myself, *if anyone is going to say anything nice about Suzette, I guess it has to be me.* Trembling, I rose to my feet.

"I met Suzette four years ago," I said, my voice quavering. One of the brothers smirked when I said the name *Suzette.* I looked him dead in the eye as I continued to speak.

"At a time when I really needed a friend, she was there. I can't tell you how grateful I am for that. I can't begin to tell you how much my life has changed because of her. She loved me. She guided me."

My mind flashed back to the time she brought Jesse Jordan's reign of terror to an abrupt halt, and I smiled. "She protected me, when no one else would or could. She taught me so many things that helped me become who I am today."

I felt a sob welling up from my abdomen, and I choked out my last few words. "It's impossible for me to say how much Suzette meant to me. She's not here anymore, but she'll be with me in spirit. Forever."

Then I collapsed in my chair, my body shaking, tears streaming down my face. My mother slid her thin arm around my shoulders and held me tightly. "That was beautiful, honey," she whispered.

Suddenly, I heard someone behind me speaking. I glanced over my shoulder and saw that a woman had risen to her feet. "I'm Suzette's friend Shirley," she said. "I had the privilege of being close to Suzette during the last year of her life. She meant the world to me. She was one of the most loving people I've ever known."

I searched my heart for any remnants of jealousy toward the woman who'd been one of the people to replace me as Suzette's center of attention. I found none. I was just happy that one more person could express appreciation for our departed friend.

Then, one by one, Suzette's disheveled bar friends rose to their feet, bravely mumbling a sentence or two.

"Suzette was a really good person," said a straggly-haired young man in ragged blue jeans. "There aren't many people in this world who are as good as she was."

"I'll never forget what she did for me," sniffled a heavily made-up woman wearing a too-tight tee shirt.

"I trusted her," said a snaggle-toothed older man who respectfully removed his stocking cap and held it in his rough hands. "I knew she'd never do me wrong."

On they continued. "She was someone I could always count on." "She was really smart. She always gave me good advice." "She was there for me during one of the hardest times of my life."

I looked over at the brothers. Their eyes were downcast, their faces somber. I hoped they were feeling ashamed.

CHAPTER 38

Suzette's funeral gave me a degree of closure, and afterwards, I felt better. But a lingering question nagged at me, burning a hole in my heart. *Had I let Suzette down?*

I'd wanted her to know that our friendship had endured even when we were apart, that my love had come through for her at the end. Had she been aware of the fact that I'd rushed to the hospital to be by her side? Or had she thought she was dying alone? After her insatiable, life-long quest for love and attention, I couldn't bear the thought of Suzette feeling lonely in her last moments.

On the evening of my birthday, two-and-a-half weeks after the funeral, the weather was unseasonably warm for November. Thunderstorms had been forecast for the night, and the atmosphere felt troubled and unsettled. I was too restless to focus on anything. I couldn't concentrate enough to read, and when I flipped through the television channels, nothing held my interest. So I went to the kitchen to tackle a pile of dirty dishes, but the task seemed too daunting.

For several minutes, I paced back and forth in my living room, occasionally stopping to peer out the window into the uneasy darkness, watching flashes of lightning on the faraway horizon. Finally, I went to bed, and with thunder rumbling in the distance, I fell into an agitated sleep.

I was jolted awake by the sound of the radio alarm clock on my nightstand. I checked the time. It was only 11:00 PM. *I'm sure I set the alarm for 7:00 AM,* I told myself. *Why is it going off now?* I switched the alarm off, and then tossed and turned before falling back into a restless sleep.

At 2:00 AM, I sat bolt upright in bed when I was again awakened by the sound of the radio. "This is too weird!" I said aloud, a chill creeping through my body. "What the heck is going on?"

Afraid to fall asleep again, I lay wide awake, staring into the darkness, waiting for daylight to come.

But I must have fallen asleep again, against my will. I really don't know whether I was sleeping and dreaming, or whether I was awake and having a vision. All I know is that Suzette came to me.

Her figure was stately, luminous, and magnificent. Surrounding her in the darkness were countless points of sparkling light that bathed her form in a white glow.

"Suzette!" I exclaimed.

"Lanie." Her voice was melodic, peaceful.

Even in my altered state of consciousness, I was aware that I'd been granted a window of opportunity to ask a question, and I was determined to seize it. "Suzette, did you know I was there at the hospital when you died? Did you know I came to be with you?"

"Yes." Her single syllable was like a musical note.

I waited for her to say more, to express gratitude for my loving deed. But I sensed she was in a state of being where such gestures were no longer relevant. She was beautiful, she was perfect. She no longer needed anyone to love her. She was the essence of love itself. She had no need for anything at all, and there was nothing I could give her. Her visit was for my sake.

And then I saw a familiar face behind her, peering over her shoulder. It was a face I'd seen only in a photo, a dark-haired, dark-eyed man. He was smiling at me, holding a bouquet of bright pink roses. Suzette had brought him with her, as her final gift to me.

Then I felt the love surrounding me, Suzette's love, my father's love, all the love streaming from those myriad points of light, bathing me in an essence I'd never felt before, a harmonic hum of unspeakable bliss.

All that love, just for me.

Every cell of my body wept tears of joy and gratitude, which poured from my eyes, running down my face, soaking my pillow. When I returned to my normal waking state, I lay unable to move for a few minutes, my body sizzling with pure white energy.

CHAPTER 39

Nana died in December of last year, just two months after Suzette passed. She suffered a massive stroke and was gone within hours.

My mother and I clung to one another during the difficult times that followed. We told each other we were glad Nana didn't have to suffer long, as she never could have borne the indignity of infirmity and dependence. We made sure she had an elaborate service at St. Augustine's Episcopal Church, just the way she would have wanted it. It seemed like half the county showed up, filling all the pews in the small church plus the chairs set up in the aisles and along the back.

My mother and I have had many long conversations about Nana and her influence on our lives. Once, my mother forgot herself and said, "It's kind of a relief not to have to hold my breath all the time, waiting for her to criticize me." Then she looked stricken by her own outspokenness. "But I miss her, Elaine. I really do."

"I miss her, too," I said. I decided not to admit to the fact that I can also breathe more freely now that Nana's overbearing presence has been removed from my life. I constantly tell my mother I'm so glad I still have her, and she says the same to me. We relate to each other in a new way, a deeper way.

It's odd. As much as I dream about Suzette, I haven't dreamed about Nana once since she died. Frankly, I prefer it that way. Someday, I may be ready for a dream visit from her, but not just yet.

But I love Suzette's dream visits. She's never again appeared as a glowing figure bringing me all the love in the universe. However, she's always healthy and vibrant in my dreams, with strong legs. Once, she came dancing into a room where I was sitting, pirouetting like a ballerina.

Sometimes when I'm working on my sculpting, or when I'm seated at my meditation table, I feel Suzette's presence near me. It reminds me of what she used to say about her spirit guides. Maybe it's just my imagination, because I associate sculpting and meditating with her. But I like to think she's there, looking out for me.

My mother looks as if she's had an enormous weight lifted off her shoulders. She's in her fifties now, but she seems younger and prettier than she did twenty years ago. A week after the funeral, she went to the salon and had her mousy, gray-streaked hair dyed blonde. The color looks great on her.

I convinced her to throw out her baggy old brown sweaters and everything else in her wardrobe that was drab and shapeless. Then we went shopping at the mall in Columbus, and I coached her in buying outfits that flatter her slender figure, stylish things in vibrant colors. She looks like a million bucks now, no longer the aging spinster.

And then she started dating, which absolutely blew my mind. Her boyfriend, Calvin, is ten years her junior. He calls her *Vivvy*, which makes her smile. No one has ever called her by a pet name before.

Nana's house and money are in my mom's name now, and some people say that's what Calvin is after. But my mom's not worried about that. She's having a great time with him. He took her on a trip to Disney World, and she can't stop talking about that experience. It was on Nana's money, of course, but that doesn't make any difference to her.

Calvin is a bushy-haired, dark-eyed fellow with a southern drawl more pronounced than that of most Brown County residents. Half of the time, I can't make out what he's saying. Maybe he's from Kentucky. I don't know. I haven't asked.

Calvin certainly isn't an intellectual kind of guy, but he's a good, steady worker, and when it comes to doing things around my mother's house, he's brilliant. He's tackled all kinds of repairs Nana let slide the last few years of her life.

He helped my mom strip the old floral wallpaper out of the living room. Then they painted the walls bright yellow and hung some posters they bought on their trip. My mom's decorating taste runs along Disney themes now. Not to my liking, but it's her life, not mine.

Last week when I stopped by the house, I could hear Calvin banging around in the basement. My mom told me he was fixing the furnace.

"You're really into this guy, aren't you, Mom?" I said

She gave me a shy grin and spread out her arms, palms up, in a gesture of cluelessness. "What can I say?" she said in her soft little voice. "The man turns me on."

I'd never before heard my mother utter words like that. I howled with laughter, and she laughed along with me. I couldn't stop laughing, and I was afraid Calvin would hear us and come upstairs. So I covered my mouth with my hand and ran out of the house, then sat in my car, laughing so hard my stomach hurt. I still laugh every time I think about it.

I'm so happy for her.

Kevin came by my office for a massage the other day. It was weird having him in the house as a client rather than a husband, and I was pretty sure he was there for reasons other than his sore pitching shoulder. During the massage, he told me that he and Jessica had split up because she was having an affair with another man. He seemed to expect sympathy, and

I had to bite the inside of my cheek to keep from laughing at the irony of the situation.

At the end of the appointment, he lingered awkwardly, like he had something else he wanted to say. But I didn't encourage him. I wasn't at all tempted to go back down the old road with him.

Finally, he asked, "You seeing anybody?"

I smiled. I could have told Kevin that I know all about chemistry now.

Because two weeks after Suzette's death, I received the shock of my life. Ken Perry called me.

"I just wanted to see how you're doing," he said, "and to apologize for how I acted in the hospital. I left abruptly, and afterwards, I realized I'd been rude. You were in a difficult position, and I'm sure you could've used a little support."

"Thank you," I said. "Apology accepted. I'm just grateful for what you did when you called your dad to get information about Suzette's family."

Surprisingly, we talked for an hour after that, about what had happened between his father and Suzette, and her downhill slide at the end.

That was seven months ago, and Ken and I have been talking ever since. More than talking, actually. You could say we're a couple now.

Ken may be an introverted fellow, but I've discovered so much beneath his quiet surface. It's true what they say about still waters. Ken has his own brand of charm, and I'll have to say, I'm hooked on it.

We've laughed about that Thanksgiving Day four-and-a-half years ago, when Suzette's attempt to hook us up backfired. She had the right idea all along. But like she told me, love has its own timing.

And she was right about another thing. I'm thriving in a relationship where I'm number one in my man's life. Ken never lets me forget that I'm his top priority.

I've seen Eldon a few times since I started dating Ken. He lives in Franklin now. It's weird to see him in his tiny apartment instead of a big house with a garage. I feel sorry for him, but he doesn't indulge in self-pity.

I asked him what he did with all his woodworking tools. "They're in storage," he said. "Maybe someday, I'll have a place where I can use them again."

He told me he's forgiven Suzette for what she did to him. "She was a free spirit," he said. "She was interesting, that's for sure. But that kind of person can be hard to live with sometimes."

Eldon still likes to hug me, but Ken won't put up with too much of that. He says, "Enough already, Dad!"

The last time Ken and I visited Eldon, he told us he was dating someone. I couldn't resist teasing him. "Is she a free spirit like Suzette?"

He grinned and shook his head. "One of those in a lifetime is enough."

But my ex-husband didn't need to know all this. "Yes," I told Kevin. "I'm seeing somebody now."

"Okay, then." He picked up my business card from the stack on my desk and stared at it, squinting. "You changed your name?"

"Yes."

"How's come?"

I just smiled and shrugged. Kevin stuffed the card in his wallet and ambled out the door.

He didn't need to know I've finally figured out it isn't that difficult to be who you really want to be.

To do what you really want to do.

To define yourself in any way you choose.

My business card now says *Lanie Rose* instead of *Elaine Greene.* I decided that if I was going to be identified with a color, it might as well be my favorite color, a rich, vibrant pink.

So a few months ago, I went down to the courthouse in Nashville and had my name changed, simple as that.

My new last name is also the name of my favorite flower, and the corner of my business card is now embossed with a single, bright pink rose.

OTHER BOOKS BY LOIS JEAN THOMAS

Me and You—We Are Who? (The Sambodh Society, Inc., 2006)

All the Happiness There Is (The Sambodh Society, Inc., 2006)

Johnny and Kris (The Sambodh Society, Inc., 2013)

Daughters of Seferina (CreateSpace, 2013)

Days of Daze: My Journey Through the World of Traumatic Brain Injury (CreateSpace, 2014)

Rachel's Song (CreateSpace, 2014)